Praise for *The Off-Season*:

"Wholly atmospheric, *The Off-Season* draws you into its unsettling world and keeps you there. I devoured it." **Jennie Godfrey, author of *The List of Suspicious Things***

"Moody, atmospheric and with an eeriness that creeps up on you like the tide!" **Anna Bailey, author of *Tall Bones***

"Time spent waiting for a funeral takes a sinister turn. An intriguing and surprising novella, simultaneously nightmarish and uplifting - it chills and invigorates, like an off-season seafront." **Alison Moore, author of the Man Booker-shortlisted *The Lighthouse* and *The Retreat***

"With its fragile, fracturing characters and chilly seaside liminality, *The Off-Season* plots a careful course between macabre and heartbreaking." **Charlotte Tierney, author of *The Cat Bride***

"*The Off-Season* is a delightfully tense haze of despair, doused in regret and drenched in the unsettling, bleak atmosphere of a Blackpool winter. I don't know whether to feel comforted or chilled by the end but I know one thing: I *need* to read it again soon." **Katherine Silva, author of *Undead Folk***

"In this darkly glittering fairground ride of a novella, Robins brilliantly evokes the haunting atmosphere of a dying seaside resort...You won't be able to help being swept along." **Megan Taylor, author of *The Therapist's Daughter***

"There's magic in this captivating novella... Robins has a lot to say about family and community." **Laura Pearson, author of *Missing Pieces***

The Off-Season

Jodie Robins

Wild Hunt Books

The Off-Season
First published in 2025 by Wild Hunt Books
wildhuntbooks.co.uk

This novel is entirely a work of fiction. The names, characters and incidents portrayed in it are the work of the author's imagination. Any resemblances to actual persons, living or dead, events or localities are entirely coincidental.

A CIP catalogue record for this title is available from the British Library

Paperback: 978-1-7394580-8-9
Ebook: 978-1-7394580-9-6

Cover Design by Luísa Dias
Edited by Ariell Cacciola
Typeset by Wild Hunt Books

The Northern Weird Project is a registered trademark of Wild Hunt Books

For Mum

To the Café

Tommy walks along the empty promenade. It's early morning, the town mostly still sleeping, only stragglers doing their walk of shame in the distance. They pay him no attention. He passes the biggest gift shop on the Blackpool seafront, some two or three shops wide, garish and loud, regardless of the season. Today, the plastic windmills race each other in the brisk Irish Sea winds, and Tommy looks at the nameless woman sitting behind the counter. She is wrapped up to the chin, her fingers flicking the pages of a magazine. She continues to turn the pages even as she looks at Tommy, with no recognition on her face. Tommy glances up and down the empty promenade and silently wishes her a fruitful day before heading to the café.

Behind him, he can hear the tinny music from the pier speakers, the robotic, maniacal laugh that belongs to some arcade game or other, one he hasn't played since he was a kid. Music and sounds that play only to themselves this January morning. And the roar of the swirling sea, never silent, no matter the weather.

Summer is an age ago, forgotten between months that fall dark and heavy. These long days that don't remember the feel of the sun, the tourists in shorts and vests and bare feet, the screams of children and the sweet sickliness of all the sugary over-indulgence. Tommy lost the magic of the place somewhere back in the 90s when childhood naivety had left him.

From inside the café he can hear the morning chatter, the window steamed with all their hot breaths on the cold glass. Tommy looks down at his black trousers, his black suit jacket, his wonky tie, and pushes open the door.

Tommy boy! Pat shouts from behind the counter, the permanent grin painted on his face.

Pat, Tommy nods in his direction, their daily routine in full action.

Usual?

Ta

Tommy pulls his chair from under his usual table and sits, waiting for his dad, Al, to lift his eyes from his copy of *The Daily Mail*.

Morning, Dad. Everything alright?

His dad shakes the page, lifting the corner that's drooped.

All good, Son, you?

You remember what day it is?

'Course

Tommy looks at his dad in his knitted jumper, his hair dishevelled from the wind.

Pat places a mug of tea on the table.

Bacon sarnie on its way

Thanks. Then, tipping the sugar into the brew, *Sad day*

Pat pushes his hands into the pocket of his apron. *Sure is. Thought he had a bit longer with us, to be honest.* He looks out the window, deep in thought, and Tommy wonders what he can see through the steamed glass. Pat sighs. *Good man, our Joe*

The regulars, faces he spends most mornings with, bang their fists on the tables in agreement, nods accompanying. Tommy smiles in that sad way he's recently learnt, this being the third funeral of the year and January not yet over. Sheila and George, B&B owners since Tommy could remember, smile back at him, resigned to the situation, knowing more might die before the year is out. At least, that's what their faces say. He wonders if they know they have merged into one another, grey-speckled hair cut to the chin, black-framed glasses hiding eye bags, their movements in unison. On the table next to them, David and Mark turn their heads to catch the radio forecast, the newest additions to their group, and still a bit of an enigma to Tommy. New Blackpool, his dad always calls them, those who came for the laughs but got sucked into the town's under-belly. He still isn't sure what they do all day.

Bloody weather, David says, and Mark rubs the back of his hand, as Tommy has seen him do many times.

Joe won't care, Mark says. *He'd be mad if the sun came out*

You're right, Mark. This is a good day for him. George's voice booms, making Tommy blink.

In the far corner, her back against the damp window, sits Alicia. The oldest. The most watched over. She grins at Tommy and pulls a deck of cards from her pocket.

Pick a card, she says, her thick Northern Irish voice now a croak.

Tommy leans back in his chair and reaches his hand out, pulling a card loose from her ridiculous grip.

Make it easier, Alicia, he laughs before looking down at the nine of diamonds and sliding it back into the pack. He turns away, pretending he has no idea how this trick will go.

Is your card the nine of diamonds?

It is! How'd you do that?

A magician never reveals her tricks, she taps the end of her nose. Alicia was never a magician. She worked in the laundrette most of her life, folding bedsheets until her hands no longer worked.

Why are you dressed for a funeral? she says, scowling.

It's Joe's funeral today. Remember?

Oh yes, of course! Then she looks down at her black dress. *See, I'm already dressed for it*

Again, Tommy forces the sad smile. *You're all good, Alicia.* She sits back and sips her tea. David watches her like you might watch a toddler, his eyes constantly sliding between her and whoever else he's talking to. Tommy likes this about David. The fatherly quality. His own dad is yet to lift his eyes.

Anything interesting going on in the world, Dad? Tommy slurps his tea.

His dad grumbles something under his breath. Tommy doesn't catch it but knows he's probably talking about the state of his country. He wonders often if this is something that comes with age. The moaning. The lack of anything good in the world. As he glances round, he sees his own future. Like God's own waiting room. Picked off one at a time, sometimes out of sequence, out of an order that feels right.

Take his own ma, for example. Gone five years now. Just 65. The shift in his dad. Tommy knows his dad has gone to the place in his head where all he was waiting for was his own demise. It seems to Tommy that coming home hadn't been enough of a replacement and still the biggest part of his dad had died that day.

How's tricks then, Tommy? David says. *Any news on the job front?*

Al looks up now, his eyebrow raised in its usual way. Tommy looks away.

Nothing so far, David. I have to say, this winter has felt long. Looking forward to spring, to being first in line

David laughs. *You and every other bugger*

Should have got your taxi licence, like I said five years ago, Al says, back to scanning the pages of doom.

Tommy could think of nothing worse than ferrying the Blackpool stags and hens everywhere, cleaning vomit from the cab, because working nights was the most lucrative. It's why his dad will amble home soon and sleep the day away. After Joe's funeral, he hopes.

Shouldn't you be retiring soon, Al? David shouts like he's talking to someone who is hard of hearing.

Al barks a laugh and leaves it there.

Alicia is wiping the window by her head, but it soon steams up again.

Pat puts the bacon sandwich in front of Tommy.

Cheers

He takes a bite, the undercooked fat pulling out from the bread, long and stringy. Tommy plays with it in his fingers before shoving the entire side of fat in his mouth and chewing until he can chew no more and all that is left to do is swallow.

Not having breakfast, Dad?

Already had a plate. Some of us have been here since dawn

Pat throws Tommy a look, a roll of the eyes that says ignore him.

Here, Al, Pat says, *what are your thoughts on the new supermarket that's going up?*

Tommy takes another bite, looks at his dad who sits up and back in his chair, folding his arms.

Well, completely pointless, I'd say. It's not a cheap one, so who round here can afford to shop there anyway? And we've lost a car park for it. Supposed to be a town for tourists. It's no good if they can't park anywhere

These are the most words he'd heard his dad say in weeks. And he wonders then if the weather bothers him more than he realises.

Oohh, Alicia says behind Tommy. He cranes his neck to look at her, but she's still rubbing the window with her hand, trying to catch a glimpse of something outside.

Alright there, Alicia? David says.

She laughs, rubbing again at the window.

Pat walks forward from behind the counter and leans against the wall, crossing one of his long legs over the other. *Now, listen. Obviously I can't come and say my farewell to Joe today, I have nobody to watch this place.* Tommy catches a raised eye from George to Sheila. *But I've known that lad for thirty years or more, and I'll miss him like hell. I want you all to have a drink for him on me.* He passes Tommy a twenty-pound note. *And tell him I'll be having one of my own for him later*

Tommy nods, feeling a knot in his throat, which he tries to swallow away. Other people's sadness, always becoming a burden of his own. His dad has closed his paper and sits with his hands folded in his lap, his face blank.

Alright, Dad?

Fine, Son

Looking up at Pat, Tommy says, *I'll make sure we all give him a good send off*

Pat nods. *Let's make this the last one for a while, hey?*

Tommy wonders who might have to die before he closes the café. He imagines he might be way down that list. Alicia, maybe.

But he shakes his head, ridding himself of the morbid thoughts that have been creeping for weeks now. The feeling that time was running out. The knowledge that for so many, it already had. Forty-two. He's only forty-two. Still. No wife, not anymore. No kids. Never got round to that. And what kind of grandpa would his dad have been? Might that have given him more to smile about?

Pulling his cigarettes from his pocket, he stands and goes outside. He keeps his head down, disappearing under the shelter of the closed down video store, and flicks his lighter to the end, inhaling. Across the road, he sees a woman and child, no older than seven. *Say cheese!* Her kid forces something clown-like onto his face, something a little demonic that spreads from ear to ear. They move along the empty prom, their hair whipping their faces so all they can do is push it back. Tommy feels cold just looking at them.

He looks away, up the coast, the giant glitter ball peeking just over the parapet. Not so sparkly anymore, more a dull sheen. Then he looks back at the off-season tourists, wondering why the boy isn't in school and wondering, for the millionth time, why the hell they want to come here in January.

'Cause it's cheap son, Ma always said. *Might be the only holiday a kid gets,* and then Tommy would walk off with guilt in his cold bones.

Ma was Blackpool. Tommy never felt like he was.

The mum repositions the boy, telling him to stand up straight. Tommy knows the Tower will be in the background. Memory making. No matter if it's a good memory or not.

Tommy stubs out the cigarette and bends his head against the onslaught of wind, pushing through the door and back into the warmth.

Say bloody cheese! He hears her yell as the door closes behind him.

Alicia is still glued to the window, looking the other way, up to the north, maybe at Central Pier that sang its lonely tunes to Tommy earlier.

Alicia, more tea? Pat calls.

She waves her hand at him dismissively and Pat shrugs. Alicia laughs again.

Son?

Tommy sits down.

Yes, Dad

I've been going through some things. Clearing some bits out. Tommy feels his heart drop in his chest.

Yeah?

You know, I read about this Swedish approach where it's not good to leave everything for your kids to do when you're gone, and that you should pass things on while you're still here to do it. Like a cleanse, sort of thing

Oh God, Dad. What are you saying?

I'm not saying anything, he flicks his fingers in annoyance. *Other than that, I started. Photos, mementos, some of your mum's things that you might want. Paperwork in order. I've got my funeral all paid for, too*

Tommy looks around and he sees Sheila, cup halfway to her lips, George, forever scowling, David and Mark, smirking, all watching them, their mouths open. Pat is mid-turn of the bacon, tongs in hand. Behind them, Alicia laughs.

Would you look at that, she says. They all glance at her, but whatever she is seeing is not as interesting as what his dad is spilling in front of them all. Acknowledgement, finally, that he wants to be gone. That he sees it happening soon.

Dad, I don't think I like this, Tommy whispers.

Unfortunately, Son, it's just a part of life we all need to face up to

But there's nothing wrong with you

There was nothing wrong with Joe, either, until there was

George coughs and Sheila scowls.

Dad

My God, I'm not saying I'm dying. I'm saying I'm getting things in order. It feels good, actually. Like I have a bit of control. I'd like you to come round and see what you want

Is there a lot? Tommy envisions boxes and boxes of his childhood and his tiny bedsit that can barely contain his own scant belongings.

No, not a lot

He isn't sure if he should be upset by this. A lifetime that amounts to not a lot.

Not a lot, Alicia cackles, and Tommy winces. *Wonder if it's more than that lot are wearing?*

What lot? What ARE you on about, Alicia? David pushes his chair back, his voice a squeak that sends a bolt down Tommy's neck. His dad is looking at him, his eyes soft, like he hasn't just set in motion the beginning of his end, and Tommy feels his cheeks colour under his dad's scrutiny, under Sheila's eyes, Pat's burning bacon.

Can we talk about this later? At home? Tommy whispers.

Of course, Son

David is squeezing past them, his red and black polka dot shirt brushing Tommy's elbow. He gives Tommy a wink as if to say he knows how shit that conversation must have been. As shit as that shirt, Tommy thinks.

Not really funeral attire, that, David

No, David smiles, *but Joe would appreciate it. Right, Alicia, what is all this commotion coming from you?* David sweeps his hand across the window, clearing a big area, and peers through, his nose close to the cold glass. And he starts to laugh. He puts his hands on his hips.

What is it? Mark says, smiling at the spectacle of his boyfriend leaning over the laughing body of Alicia, her shoulders rising and falling with each guffaw.

You gotta see this, David says, now resting his hand on Alicia's shoulder.

Right bunch of loons, Alicia shouts.

And with that, Sheila stands, almost sending her chair flying, and George follows her. Pat skips past the tables, and Mark pushes himself up on his dodgy hip. Tommy watches as each arrives at the window. Gasps and laughs. Except now, they all fill the window and Tommy can't see anything except the backs of their heads. He stands and heads for the door, turning back to his dad saying, *Are you coming?*

Al shakes his head and opens up the paper again as Tommy pulls open the door and walks outside.

There, just past the café, on the other side of the road, chugs a black bus, fumes billowing, open top, huge wheels. The bus is stuffed full of people. Bodies like sardines in a tin, limbs extended, twisted. Each visible face wearing a huge smile. Bikini tops, trunks, hair tied in buns. All dressed as if it were the height of the warmest summer.

Tommy pulls his jacket across his body. The blackness of the bus a thing of distinct ugliness, out of place even on this dreary seafront, something about it a little bit evil looking. He pokes his head back inside the door, looks at his friends huddled at the window. *This lot are mental! And what kind of bus is that?*

A charabanc, Alicia proclaims.

A what? David says.

Al stands and walks towards Tommy, peering around the door.

My God. The woman's right! A charabanc. Like an old bus that used to ferry tourists to the seaside. Never have I seen one with my own eyes

Tommy sees Al shiver, his eyes firmly on the bus, and Tommy feels the same cold engulf him, a cold from under the skin.

And from the charabanc, a shrill shriek of excitement before the travellers one-by-one climb down and step bare foot onto the cold, damp promenade.

Travellers Descend

TOMMY STANDS IN THE open doorway. His friends inside the café are chattering even louder than when Tommy arrived. Alive, suddenly. Cackles, like witches, intersperse their insults of the travellers who have congregated across the road.

His dad is leaning against the doorframe, wedging the door open with his foot, his arms folded. Tommy sees in him a curiosity as he watches the travellers organise themselves, an innocence, something child-like. For fear of breaking the spell, Tommy says nothing.

It feels to him as if his own childhood was both yesterday and a hundred years ago. He was raised in a north shore ground floor flat, two-bedrooms, one lounge that looked over the busy road, one very tiny kitchen where you couldn't swing a turnip, and a concrete backyard shared with the various people who lived upstairs. Some of those people have faded to blank faces, but some are so vivid, Tommy would know them instantly. Then he realises that they are most likely long dead.

Those days are hazy, and he seemingly can only conjure the sunny days, the never-ending summer days that stretched like the promenade, a beautiful, sweeping thing that allowed the entire front to be visible. The colours so vibrant, the sounds never once annoying or disorienting, and he thinks that this is a good thing. Happy, he must have been.

But Al is now looking at the travellers with disgust, no happy memories there for him, and he shrugs his shoulders against the cold, bends his head, and goes back inside.

Al checks his watch, a 60th birthday present from Ma.

Tea, please Pat, and Tommy sees him shiver as he sits back down.

He lays out his coins on the table, the same way he does every time. He looks up at Tommy, *Are you good? Want more?*

Tommy nods, *Yeah, I'll have another,* so Al doubles the coins and gives Pat two fingers.

*Oh, Tommy boy, the pipes, the pipes are calling...*Pat sings from the back and Tommy shifts in his seat, a flicker of a smile on his dad's lips.

Flat as a pancake there, Pat, Al calls over his shoulder.

Ah, Jesus, you know I used to be a choirboy? Years ago, I'll grant you, but still. I wasn't tone deaf then, so doubt I am now

Well maybe my ears are flat

His dad laughs and it makes Tommy smile. A sound he is very unused to.

Al, have you ever been on one of these bus things? David says, pointing out the window.

Cheeky bugger, no, of course not. I'm not 120 years old

Well, I don't know, do I? I'm from the age of the internet

Yeah, and look where that's got you

Dad, Tommy whispers.

Not a worry, Tommy. We can't all be cab drivers. David looks back out the window, resting his elbow on Alicia's shoulder.

His dad is grinning still, except now the sweet innocence of a few moments ago has vanished.

Deckchairs! Alicia proclaims. *Red and white stripes and all,* she laughs.

As if anybody is going to be sitting out in this bloody weather, Pat shouts.

Maybe they're here for a weird, arty photo shoot or something? Mark says, his voice a soft whisper that matches his soft body. Tommy has never seen a man so soft, in fact. Like the man from the mint advert, and Tommy chuckles to himself. His dad gives him a funny look. He clears his throat, *Wouldn't be the first time people came to exploit the place, Mark*

In the dead of winter? Someone's being exploited, but it's not us. You will not believe what some of them are wearing. He walks back to his seat, his gait a little uneven, like his body told him he'd stood too long. Tommy has never known Mark's age – Mark will never tell. But the tightness in his cheeks, his attempt to stay young, points to him being at least fifty.

Barely a thread on them! Alicia says.

Tommy stands and his dad gives him a sly wink.

No. Nothing like that, Dad. Just intrigued

Uh-huh, he opens the paper to the racing pages.

Moving to the window, Tommy nudges David to the side, and a whiff of stale cologne hits him.

Out last night, were you David?

David grins. *I was*

Not been to bed?

I have not

And it's then that Tommy smells the unwashed breath, the cigarettes, the alcohol that is still as strong as if he'd just swallowed it. Tommy takes a step away.

To be out all night, to still be wearing the same clothes as the day before, the same underwear, he doesn't even remember doing that as teen, when Blackpool was still alive.

Mark shakes his head. *Just him, let me point out. Some of us have grown up a bit*

I'm more intrigued about where he went, Tommy says. *Everything I hear is that town is dead, like*

It's who you know, David says. *And who says I was out in town?*

Well, weren't you? Mark says, his voice now a little higher.

Oh, come on. None of this is new information. You used to come with me until you got boring. We USED to be the hottest couple in town!

Mark visibly prickles and Tommy looks away, out the window, wishing he'd never said a word.

More! Alicia shouts.

And behind the charabanc, a van pulls up. All Tommy can see, though, is the group of disembarked passengers stood on the promenade, their skin already mottled from the cold, yet everyone still smiling. They are dressed in homage to the past – frilled bikinis on the women who lack the curve of the 1940s body, men in trunks so tight they might cut off blood flow. Each person a splash of bright colour against the grey backdrop.

These people are insane, Tommy whispers, more to himself than anyone else.

You placing a bet today, Al? Pat asks as he sets the teas down.

Nah. Doesn't feel right today, it being Joe's day and all

Someone might want to tell this lot out here, David points.

They don't know any better, do they? Mark says, his face still set in a frown, his cheeks coloured with anger or embarrassment.

Christ, you rattled his cage, Tommy. David laughs. *Miserable git*

Tommy leaves them to their domestic, something he is pleased he no longer has to deal with. All the arguing, the attempts to make himself bigger to the wife than she made him feel. His mates from down south, Slough to be exact, had cheered the day he finally left her. They ruffled his hair like he was a child. And when he'd said to them that he wasn't so sure it was the right decision, that he felt alone, they'd reminded him that he'd never been lonelier than when he'd lived with her. And now they all continue in Slough, regulars at the pub, heading home to their families after a long day in the factory, and Tommy is left with nothing but silence. Their lives carried on without him, and he wonders if they ever think about the man that left his abusive missus.

He tries hard to not think about her. Yet still she slides in, unbidden. Burnt food in a pan is usually the trigger, that sickly sweet smell of potatoes catching as the water boils dry. Or leaving the lid off the toothpaste. And then he wonders if she does the same with whoever she lives with now, because he knows she will be living with someone. She didn't do well on her own.

Tommy looks at his dad, and remembers that he never knew her, not in the act of knowing a person beyond the initial handshake. He is a safe space from her. And mum would have been, too. Never venturing to Tommy's home in Slough, rarely ever leaving Blackpool, except maybe to Southport for the day, or a walk through the Trough of Bowland. Rarely, mind you. And only when the weather was just right.

His dad has abandoned the racing pages and is attempting the crossword. He already seems stumped. He puts his pen down, and without lifting his eyes from the page, tears the strip off the top of the sugar sachet and pours it into his tea. Mum would have gone mad at this. She banned sugar years ago when his dad's waist started to expand. It's another shift in the father who had always complied.

Need any help?

Al stirs his tea, dragging the spoon over the lip of the mug and placing it down.

Hmm. He picks his pen back up and taps at the paper. *Example, eight letters*

Tommy searches his brain.

Specimen, Alicia shouts.

Al checks the letters. *Nice one*, he says as he fills the word in.

Tommy smiles at Alicia, but really he is gutted his brain didn't work quicker. She hasn't even looked away from the window.

Next?

His dad keeps the clue quiet, sparked himself by Alicia's audacity.

Would you look at him! She declares.

David is laughing wildly beside her and when Tommy looks at Mark, he sees disdain. He shifts in his seat uncomfortably. *Come and sit down, David.* But David ignores him.

David howls. *Here, you all need to see this! He's got a top hat on and everything. Tailcoat. Proper smarmy looking*

It's got to be for a THING then, surely, if they're rolling up in costumes. Pat is wiping down the counter, tidying away the last of the breakfast items.

Tommy looks at the clock. 10:06.

Hour and a half, guys, he declares, but nobody answers him. Shelia glances at him with a grey face.

What a sad way to go, hey?

He was warned, George says.

Warned? As in the doctors said, yes, you've caught the diabetes, now off you go, Sheila shakes her head.

Caught? You don't catch it. It's not a cold. He glares at his wife across his dried-up tinned tomatoes.

Well, you know what I mean

Not sure I do

And he did catch it. From his terrible diet

She looks then at Pat as if he is the virus. Pat scowls at her and carries on cleaning.

Nobody forced the food into his mouth, George says.

No, but maybe if temptation wasn't everywhere

And you're great at resisting it, aren't you, Sheila? Al doesn't look up from his crossword as George's words come flat and hard.

Tommy shifts in his seat and says, *Come on, guys. Not today. Joe would be so upset*

People in glass houses is all I'm saying

Not sure what you're implying there, Al, George says.

I'm not implying anything, simply stating facts that Sheila has as hard a time refusing the old whiskey as Joe had refusing the old cake and chocolate and daily fry-up and three sugars in his tea. We are none of us saints

And what's your vice, Al? George crosses his arms and glares at him.

Al pauses and Tommy knows he's pretending to think.

I'm not sure. What would you say, Tommy? Do I have any vices?

Tommy looks from his dad, to George, to Sheila, to Pat and holds his hands up.

I'm not getting involved

Ah, come on. You've known me all your life, you must have an idea of what I can't say no to?

Tommy coughs and shifts onto his other bum cheek, shaking his head.

Come on!

He swallows. *Ok, if you insist.* Sheila and George lean forward. *I'd say you're addicted to loneliness*

HA! His dad shouts. *Ridiculous answer*

But Tommy sees a flash of something there in his eyes that softened for a second, which he is sure filled very quickly with tears before he blinked them away.

So, what you mean is I don't have any vices. And I'd say I agree

No, no, no, I think Tommy is onto something here, Sheila says.

Of course you do. Misery loves company after all

Al, you really are a dick, George says, and Alicia howls with laughter behind them. Sheila strokes her husband's hand.

His dad goes back to his crossword and Tommy finally takes a breath. But the air inside now feels as cold as outside. He shakes his head at his own stupidity. Again, why didn't he just keep his mouth shut? A café on the Blackpool seafront on the day of a friend's funeral, and he spills to his dad that he thinks he's addicted to loneliness. And what does he even mean?

But he knows what he means; he has thought about it a lot lately. His dad, once the warmest person in the room, has shrunk to a bitter shell. His dad, once a craver of human company, a regular at the social club, with friends and family, now chooses to sit alone each night. His own son, who returned only for him, is turned away from the door, the only space he is willing to share is right here in this damn café filled with people who are equally shunning a happier life. He knows his dad feels safe here. He is superior to these people. He is superior to his own son.

Tommy sips his tea, hoping the moment has passed. His dad casts his eyes up and over him, scorn there in the curve of his lips.

Sorry, you were *pushing*

Al holds a hand up, a quiet shush, and it feels as if the entire world can now see and hear the awkwardness between them, the chiding of the little boy son who hasn't fulfilled his rightful place as a man. Unworthy of his attention and his emotions anymore. A giant chasm in the shape of a Formica table.

Oh my God, look at that, will ya, Alicia says, and Tommy turns to look. From the van they have pulled a wooden theatre-type structure, a red curtain fluttering in the wind. And in the hands of a man in wide trousers and braces are Punch and Judy puppets, as recognisable to Tommy as his own mother. *Punch and Judy! Oh my God*, she laughs. *When were they last around these parts?*

Tommy wants to say not since he was a kid forty years ago, but really they could have been here in the summer just gone for all he knew. Not once has he stepped foot on Blackpool beach since he returned. Not once has he played tourist in his hometown.

I need to see this, Alicia finally says, pulling on her coat. It is the coat of a movie star, a rich pink, long, gold buttons, wide lapels. And with it she matches a black velvet hat that reminds Tommy of all the girls he used to see in the early 1990s. Except on closer inspection, the coat is bobbled, the lining loose and tattered, the pockets layered with decades of finger grease. He watches Alicia stand on very unsteady legs, so much so that David holds her elbow.

You can't be going out there, Alicia. It's cold and windy, Pat says.

Oh, I am, just you watch me. I need to see what they are up to. Punch and Judy! Yes please, she laughs.

I'll go with her, don't worry, David says.

Well, if you're going, I'll go, too, says Mark. He pulls on his blue paisley jacket, complete with woollen lapels.

Don't forget Joe, Tommy says.

Who? Alicia says.

Joe, his funeral

Oh, of course. No worries there

But really, he wants to take hold of Alicia, to stop her leaving, to break this draw the travellers have suddenly cast on his friends. Or not-quite friends. Or anyway, to keep them wrapped up here inside this condensation-dripping room, their breaths a weird comfort, the outside now a strange place where odd things were happening.

She pushes past all the tables like she isn't walking on eighty-seven-year-old hips and pulls open the door. David grins as if to say this is exciting. He grabs his coat from the back of his chair and to Mark says, *Are you coming, grump?*

Mark kicks his leg out but misses and David chuckles. He follows them both out onto the windy path and down the promenade, the three following the puppet master onto the tiny strip of beach below.

Father and Son

SHEILA IS LOOKING ANYWHERE other than at George, a pout on her sour face, a silence that feels a bit deafening. When Tommy shifts in his seat, the creak makes him wince. She has seemingly not forgiven her husband for showing her up in front of everyone, making her ignorance clear for all to see, the stroke of his hand now a distant memory, and she gets back up and moves over to the window.

His dad has not said another word, instead he pretends to be making progress on the crossword. Yet Tommy can see most of the boxes are empty.

This is the life that he has come to know here. People muddling through the days, waiting for something more, for better weather, for something exciting to break the mundanity. And the smiles he sees must hardly be genuine, because soon the mask slips and he sees the truth beneath them. The unhappiness, the bitterness. The poverty that is clear in their old clothes, their slightly unwashed hair that's gone a few days longer than it should. The poking around for pennies for their brew. He'd like to say they were all rich with life, with love and family, with the little pleasures, but then he looks outside at the decay of everyone's favourite seaside town, and he knows they are not rich in life at all. Otherwise, why would they choose to spend their mornings in this draughty café, day in and day out, come rain or shine, but mostly rain.

Pat starts to whistle, 'Always Look on the Bright Side of Life', and Tommy grins when Pat winks at him. If anything, it angers Sheila more and she folds her arms, her sourness now at lemon levels.

Blackpool has become a place on pause, the heady haze of the once buzzing town now relegated to their past. Yet the people still hope that the broken, crumbling render on the derelict hotels and shops might be chipped off one day, replaced with something bright white, a lure for more than stags and hens to venture here. For the off-season to be back on again.

Tommy puts his hand to his tie, checks it is still straight.

Does this look ok, Dad?

Al takes a beat before he lifts his eyes and simply nods.

And where's yours?

Dry cleaners. It's had too many wears recently

And you think it's ok to go in a wool jumper?

If it's not, I'll go home. No skin off my nose

In his voice he hears the barbs, the harshness that is so new to Tommy, it still cuts every time.

Do you want me to stop talking to you, Dad? Is that it?

Aye. Some peace would be good. All this incessant chatter, no wonder I can't find the answers

Tommy sits back, feeling his jaw tighten, words forming on his tongue that he can't let spill because that would be the end of everything. The very idea of speaking the words leaves a coil in his stomach, reminiscent of the days he knew his ma was dying yet couldn't bring himself to speak to her. Telling himself she'd be fine, there would be time, until there was actually no time left at all and all opportunity to say *I love you* was gone.

In his eyes he feels the sting that always comes when he thinks of her. The smile, the ruffle of his hair way into his thirties, the weekly phone call because really she knew he wasn't happy and home wasn't a good place. She even knew without any words needed, and that suited Tommy. The day he told her he'd left was the day he heard a lightness come in her voice and the weekly phone calls started to slip.

He took that to mean she was content. She was no longer worried about him, and he was a grown man who could look after himself. Ma never knew that he lived off microwave meals and Diet Coke and that when he walked out of his home in Slough, he left behind the person who mothered him in many similar ways. Until she didn't.

Dad never knew anything either. He wonders if they ever spoke about him, all those miles away, over the breakfast table, sipping their morning brew and flicking the pages of the newspaper. Just as Dad still did now, alone.

His dad sniggers and Tommy looks at him.

Something funny?

Al jabs the paper, and Tommy realises he has abandoned the crossword and is reading the dreaded opinion piece. He looks at the heading – 'Will We Ever Get Back to Having a Dedicated Workforce'? Tommy sighs. The same drivel.

Dad, why do you read that shit? Really? Is this another thing that comes with age? The shift to the right. He couldn't imagine it, but then he couldn't imagine his dad would shift the way he has.

I read the truth, Son. They aren't afraid to say it how it is. Something has changed in this country. Nobody seems willing to put their shift in. Entitled

Tommy sees his dad's eyes lift to his for a second, like he is casting his net over him.

I'm not entitled, Dad

Never said you were. But I don't see you out there knocking on doors, taking whatever you can get. You know, the way I did as a young lad

Oh, here we go, Sheila says, and for a minute, Tommy has forgotten she is there, lingering at the window.

Here we go. What, Sheila?

Off you go again, ranting. I'm sick of it

You know where the door is

Dad!

Now here! George booms. *Who the hell do you think you're talking to?* George stands but his small frame makes no dent on the space around them.

Al laughs. *All's I'm saying is, she doesn't have to listen to me, if I annoy her so much. She doesn't have to be in the same space. It's a free country and Sheila is free to leave. No offence intended. So, you can sit back down.* Al gestures to George's seat and Tommy watches him hesitate, his eyes wide, nostrils flared, before he takes his seat again. For a second, Tommy expected pistols at dawn, George defending his wife's honour, his dad unable to resist. His money was on his dad, what with his disassociation from any human feeling lately. George would just be a nuisance fly he swatted dead.

The café is silent again, and Tommy can only think what Joe would have thought of today. He is ashamed, like a toe-curling embarrassment, like he might actually be the one to leave. Joe with his soft ways would have told them all to shut it, to stop with the judging. But Joe was always the target, the bullied, the tripped, the name-called. Never weak, though. A shrug was all he needed to be rid of the hurt. And never here, in this damp and draughty café. Here was his safe place, too. Where Tommy would watch him smiling and wonder why he didn't just get out of here, find somewhere soft like him.

Pat pushes his tea-towelled hand into a mug and circles back and forth, his eyes on Al. He is rhythmic, lost in some dark thought about Tommy's dad.

Just wondering if there's some medication you forgot to take today, Al? Something calming, like Valium?

The only pills I take are my vitamins, Pat

Tommy lowers his head and leans in towards his dad, and hisses, *What's got in to you today?*

Hid dad inhales, takes a beat, balls his fist and taps it gently on the table. *Nothing*, he says. *No harm intended, just messing.* He looks over at the window. *Sheila, sorry. Ignore me. Apologies, George,* he holds up his hand, and Tommy lets his shoulders drop.

Pat resumes his whistling, although now the tune is indistinguishable.

I cannot believe what I'm seeing out here, Sheila says. She taps her fingers on the glass. *Dressed like it's summer, partying like it's not the depth of winter. And there's a crowd growing, too! Where have they all come from? We only have one guest, a little old man who comes every year and watches TV in our bar all day. Never once ventures out, except maybe for a pint in the pub on the corner, although he does that less and less. He told us once why he comes, didn't he George? Something about an anniversary?*

Aye, he proposed on the pier back in 1953, or was it 54?

Sheila doesn't answer, already bored with the conversation she started. Tommy watches her as she stands on her tiptoes, unbalanced, ungainly, using the glass as support, and wonders why the B&B owners are here having breakfast instead of feeding their lone guest.

George! she shouts. *George, he's out there! Our guest is out there*

Don't be silly. And he has a name, but then Tommy sees a flash of panic on George's face before he stands up, distracting himself from his own faux pas. *Let me see*

He pushes Sheila aside and she points, *There! See. He's on the prom, grinning like a maniac, watching that man in the tall hat. George, it's weird, ain't it? I mean, what is going on?*

Just looks like good old seaside entertainment to me. I mean, look at all the equipment they are carrying down to the sand

But it's freezing!

It's not that bad. A bit of a brisk wind, slightly overcast

Brisk wind? Those flagpoles they're erecting are almost sideways

And as they stand there, a boom of music erupts from the seafront, louder than anything the piers produce, old in style, tinny, like someone might be playing a Wurlitzer. The windows rattle.

Oh, come on, no use standing in here, speculating about it. Let's go and see for ourselves, George says.

Tommy looks at Al, and his eyebrows are raised and a slight shake of the head is starting.

But the weather! Sheila says.

And Joe's funeral, Tommy says.

Ah, there's time. Just a quick look

Tommy looks at the clock. 10:20.

George picks up both of their coats and throws She-lia hers. She grumbles, pushing her arm into the sleeve, yanking her woolly hat onto her head. George pulls open the door and a surge of ear-piercing sounds flood the café, sounds that rattle the eardrum like nights in the clubs, that spike like the death cry of a seagull.

Jesus! Pat shouts and Tommy throws his hands to his ears.

Back in a few, George says with a grin, and with that, Tommy, Al and Pat are the only ones left.

You don't fancy it? Tommy says to Al with a tip of the head.

I'd rather stick pins in my eyes

Or ears, Tommy laughs.

His dad laughs and the sound is everything in that moment. Gentle over the grating screech from outside.

So, Tommy says, *you think I'm not doing enough to get a job, Dad?*

Can we not just sit in peace, Son?

I'm not after a row. I'm just asking. What would you do? If you were me?

You don't want me to answer that

I do

His dad sits back in his chair and folds his arms. He looks Tommy in the eyes and grinds his jaw, and Tommy mirrors him.

Why are you here?

What?

Why are you here? In Blackpool?

Huh, not sure I was expecting that

Pat disappears from behind the counter, and Tommy wonders if he's hiding.

No, it's not a nice question, Son, but the answer is important

I'm here for you, of course

His dad pouts.

Not necessary

Thanks

Tommy grinds his teeth until his jaw hurts, his dad watching him, challenging him to a comeback.

Did you think I needed a babysitter? His dad continues. *Is that it? Too old to tie my own laces, or something?*

Of course not. It was nothing to do with that. I came back for you so you weren't alone

Like a babysitter

For fuck's sake, Dad!

Come on boys, enough of that. Pat has reappeared, his coat thrown over the counter. *No idea what's got into you all today. Like a creche in here and I'm too bloody past it to be your minder*

No, I'm sorry, Pat, Tommy says, *he's been on one all day, he's been at me all day...*From outside the shrieks and howls seem to increase in volume, a shrillness that pierces Tommy's eardrum. He sees Pat squint, but his dad stays still and solid...*and it's not even lunchtime yet!* He points at the clock. *What is your problem? You think I'm here to look after you because you're old and past it, which isn't the case at all, yet your face says you want to punch me*

His dad shakes his head, but he can't tell if it is in disagreement or in disgust. But if nothing else, Al now seems to be enjoying this.

Tommy sips his cold tea, the dribble escaping the lip of the cup and he wipes it away with his thumb. Small things like these he has come to notice before he realises it is likely down to his boredom. He shifts in his seat, feeling a surge of energy in his legs, an urge to get up and walk. To walk away from his now miserable father, the man he finds hard to look at, because to look at him is to see the changed man he has become. Someone he mostly no longer recognises. His father is not a bad person, he knows this. His father is hurting. His father is lost, but like plunging your hand in the water to grab at something, Tommy always seems to miss when he tries to find him. He is always an inch or two further away, sliding like an eel from his clutch, determined not to be caught by the son who left and then came back. He has never felt welcomed here. Like his presence is now an annoyance, like the only thing that ever held them together, his Ma, is now gone. And so, his father slips and slides, throws sly looks his way, and there in their silence leaves Tommy to drown. The rescuer now the one needing rescue.

But then Tommy wonders why he *is* here. Why he would return to the place that only ever felt fun as a child, before the rot of the place became obvious, before the sheen had gone, before the sheer poverty and destitution of its sad-looking people was obvious on every street corner. And of course, he'd hoped to return to the place that brought him joy, that felt familiar and safe in many ways. A place where he knows who lives where, who might be selling the Gazette on the corner of Marks, the place where his wife is not.

A drum beat now, to add to the high-pitched Wurlitzer squealing, and Tommy hears his own thoughts getting bashed.

Jesus, what a racket! Pat shouts, and the windows shudder in time with Tommy's blinking.

What is this new hell? his dad says, but he doesn't move to go and look, instead he hangs his head. Tommy wonders if he might be crying, and the thought stabs him as the memory of his mum's funeral floods him. A broken man that day, and no smiles from him since. Tommy leans forward, glances at Pat, who shrugs.

Come on, Pat bangs Al on the back, *let's go see for ourselves*. But Pat's face isn't jovial anymore, he's rattled, distracted by the painful sounds seeping through the single-glazed window. There's a paleness there, a hanging jowliness likes he's lost the inclination to tighten his face. Almost like he might vomit at any moment.

I'm not going out there! Al says, almost with a laugh, his head now raised again, his eyes wide.

Well, you are, because I'm closing up

Closing up?

Al looks at Tommy now, his mouth slightly open, and the harshness in his eyes has gone, replaced with a child-like worry.

Never known you close for anything, Pat, Tommy says. *Not even a funeral*

No, I know. Pat's voice trails. *Only for a minute, like. Just to get a look for myself*

Come on, Dad. Tommy stands up.

I don't want to!

I know, but there's no choice. It's the funeral soon any-way

Still another hour

It's fine, Dad. Come on

Pat has shrugged his coat on and moved to the door. His fingers on the handle, he pulls it open, and in crashes the sounds – the drums, the Wurlitzer, the shouts of the ever-building crowd. Tommy stands in the door and looks outside. The crowd has not simply grown, it has multiplied fifty-fold. People are everywhere.

Jesus Christ, he whispers.

Where have they all come from? Were they hiding in their hotels? Pat folds his arms, and leans his head out, looking up and down the prom. *Come on*

Al gets up and stands behind them, his body small next to the bulk of Pat, and Tommy sees a frailty. *Can't believe you're closing for this madness,* he says.

Me either, Pat says, but he shuffles the two of them out and pulls the door closed, locking it shut. And Tommy sees Pat's head tilt, his mouth slightly open, eyes watching the rag-tag group, hypnotised.

The three of them stand in the doorway, huddled like penguins against the Irish Sea winds, watching the strangers, the tourists, the locals, young, old, middling, familiar and irregular, some already having shed their outer layers, as they head towards the sounds.

Dorothy

First of all, Tommy notices the wind. It stings his eyes and makes them water. The salt of the sea is as harsh as the wind, and makes him gag, reminding him of seaweed wrapped around toes and the ungodly catches of fish in Abingdon Street Market, slime and stench everywhere as his mum dragged him through each weekend. His disgust of seafood remains to this day. Another relic of Blackpool consigned to the past. The flags that have been erected flap and billow, leaning sideways. Yet those on the promenade seem oblivious to it. They walk upright, their faces to an invisible sun. Their smiles are so wide, their laughter so loud, he can see and hear them from over the wide road, from way down the prom.

He notices how they are leaching from every side road, from every front door, from every hotel. Like ants, he thinks, and imagines the travellers to be sweet smelling things. Sugar-laced doughnuts. And as was typical of his brain, he got a whiff of the doughnut as if it were right beneath his nose. A memory again from childhood, yanked from somewhere deep and recessed.

Come on, Pat says.

Tommy raises a finger, *Joe's funeral, remember?* And in his chest there is a flutter, a heavy fear that he himself will forget.

I'm not going, remember?

But you already closed the café, Pat. You might as well, now

Pat stops walking and turns back to look at his closed door. Tommy sees a confusion in his eyes, a tiny drop of his eyebrows before he smiles, '*Och, only for a minute. Not really closed. Just 'back in a few minutes' kind of thing.* And he waves his hand in a dismissal before stepping out into the road, not a single glance left or right, and Tommy loses his tall, broad body to the crowd.

Shall we? Tommy looks at his dad.

We shall not

Well, not much else to do. He glances at his watch. *Forty minutes till the funeral*

I might give it a miss. Head home, catch up on some jobs, get some sleep

Dad

Too many funerals, Tommy!

And he realises how strange it is to hear his dad use his name. Tommy. Not Son. Not the nameless child he struggles to even look in the eye now.

Ok. Ok. I get that. And I agree. Tommy pauses. *I will still need to go, though*

Of course! I'm not your keeper. You're not my watcher. We are two grown men with autonomy

Yes

But neither move. They stand there, still and solid, arms folded.

Come on, a quick squiz. Ten minutes, a bit of a laugh, and then home. Tommy touches his dad's elbow, gives it a gentle nudge, and sees the tiny withdrawal before he relents and nods. The two of them step out from under the porch of the café door, into the windy onslaught, but they step in line with the flow of the crowd, the sounds growing, the voice on a megaphone instructing everyone to *Round up! Round up!*

Tommy is transported instantly to the summer of 1992, the first year he was allowed to roam free with friends through the endless summer holiday. He had change in his pockets, some for the 2p pushers, but some for the rides at the Pleasure Beach – the Grand National, racing friends in the other car, the Wild

Mouse and the injuries it inflicted, Steeplechase where one tip could spell death – in the days when you could wander through the park without a ticket. He turns his head and in the gloom of the day, the low cloud almost touches the tip of the Big One, closed now for the off-season, and he thinks for the thousandth time that there is nothing spookier than a closed theme park. It's the silence of the place, the lack of screams, the missing screech of the wheels on metal runners, the whoosh of the cars flying above your head. Unnatural to be silent. Always a wonder to him where the screams go, sucked into the belly of the park, absorbed by the painted figures designed to freak and scare.

They keep walking, his dad silent at his side, watching those around him like they might steal his last penny, and when Tommy sees the ecstasy, he thinks he is right to be wary.

It is only as they approach the charabanc that Tommy sees the doughnut stand, the candy floss van, the ice cream man.

The charabanc is black, dented in places, well-used, the wheels large and narrow. A death trap, Tommy is sure. But his dad is stroking it with his fingertips, running his hand along the side all the way to the front, to the scroll of a name – *Dorothy*.

Tommy holds his breath as his dad places his palm flat on the white paint. *Dorothy*. His ma. Dolly to everyone who knew her. His throat tightens and he can see his dad's has too, his eyes shining now, something like a smile forming.

What do you know? he whispers.

Ok, Dad?

Fine, Son

I'll bet she's reliable, he says, lifting his head to the driver who is sitting with his feet on the dash. The man is small, rugged, deep crevices in his skin that point to a life spent in all weathers, curly hair in need of a good wash.

Has been so far. Just requires regular maintenance. A bit more now she's so old

Don't we all, Al laughs, and Tommy is surprised by the natural sound of it.

Fancy a look?

His dad's eyes widen, *You bet I do*, and out opens the door to the roofless bus. Convertible, Tommy wonders, and checks the back for a retracted roof, but sees nothing.

What happens if it rains?

We get wet, the driver laughs.

Al has climbed up into the bus and is walking down the centre aisle, smiling. He sits and shuffles along to the edge, looking down at Tommy.

You can smell the history, feel it in the leather seats. Like stepping back in time

But you've never seen one?

No. But everyone here knows they used to line up along the front, parked for the day like coach trips, back when the hoards used to come. And my god did the hoards come! That beach would be full from prom to water, you couldn't move! Even in my youth. Well, god, even in yours! Remember? Deckchairs everywhere, promenade full to bursting, all the big names filling the theatres and the piers. It's how people travelled for seaside trips, before cars were everywhere. Before travel to warmer countries was possible. Al shakes his head.

It's still a popular place, though, Dad. People love coming to Blackpool. Reminds them of their own childhoods

Not the same though, is it? Like the magic has gone. And Tommy wonders then if the magic was Ma, and if a place loses the centre of someone's universe, then maybe it becomes as barren as the moon. His dad shrugs, resigned to living without the magic.

The driver stands up and leans back on the dash, a cigarette hanging from his mouth. He is half-grinning, half-scowling, showing his black teeth, before he inhales and squeezes his eyes shut against the smoke.

Magic has gone, you say?

The man looks around at the dads carrying children on their shoulders, at the elderly shuffling their way beside sons and daughters, grandchildren. Families, with bounce, not a creak of cold bones in sight. In fact, the closer Tommy looks, the more skin he sees. The rolled flesh, the taut, the wrinkled. Not a single care among them.

Are you a tour company, or something? Tommy says.

Could say that, he smiles, but it doesn't quite reach his eyes. *But we ain't one for booking*

Tommy shakes his head, opens his mouth, but before he can speak, the driver squeezes the black rubber horn by his side, the honk so loud it makes Tommy and Al jump and yell. The man is laughing, his dad is grimacing, but he pushes himself up and heads for the door. *Thank you,* he says as he slides past the man now blowing cigarette smoke in his dad's face.

Come on, Dad, Tommy gives him his hand as he climbs down, and the driver sits back in his seat, his feet back up on the dash.

This was a mistake, these people don't make me feel good, Al says as they walk away. But Tommy sees him glance back at his ma's name.

That guy was strange, Tommy agrees.

It's all strange

And Tommy can't disagree. The throng of people is like a wave moving them forward, towards the steps and down to the beach below, barely a sliver of sand as the tide slowly pulls out.

Shall we look for Alicia? For David and Mark? Tommy says.

Why? You really are a bit of a mother hen aren't you? Joe's funer...

Yes, yes. We all know it's Joe's funeral. You've reminded us enough times

Tommy lowers his head. *It's important*

Is it? Is it actually? A room full of upset people, forced to look at a coffin, forced to hear the cries of mourners. It's such an outdated tradition! I'd be happy to just be cremated alone and have you all gather to celebrate! His voice was rising. *I'll be dead, I'll have no idea who is there and who isn't. You don't even need to celebrate, just take yourself off somewhere quiet, say goodbye in your own way, grieve in your own way. It's torture, sitting through a funeral! Unnecessary torture!*

They continue walking and Tommy looks around to see if anyone has reacted to his dad's outburst, but they are all so focussed on getting where they are going, in having a good time, they bump into him and he staggers. Al reaches out a hand to steady him.

Mind yourselves! he yells. *No bloody manners, any of you!*

Calm down, Dad. No harm done. People are just excited

And then he looks up at the grey sky, the drizzle, and wonders what he is missing.

Let's look for Alicia

He feels a knot in his stomach, a growing unease, and when he looks back over his shoulder to the charabanc, he sees the driver watching him, tipping his black cap to him. Tommy turns away and thrusts himself into the thickening crowd, his dad now a few steps ahead of him. He reaches his hand past a stranger, a man with a wide grin and sunglasses, but his dad is just out of reach. The man shouts to someone next to him and his hot, coffee-stenched breath lands clean on Tommy's cheek. He turns away and pushes forward, reaches his dad, and the two of them descend the steps down to the beach.

His black shoes sink into the wet sand and he sighs, noting they will need cleaning before the funer…He stops himself. His dad is looking at him and, as if reading his mind, gives a little shake of the head.

He wants to say to his dad that Joe deserves a good send-off, that he was one of the good ones, less inclined to selfishness, the kind to drop everything to help. A good, solid life. A Blackpool life, close to those in need, of which there are many. He hopes his funeral will be full to bursting, but in reality, most of Joe's friends have already left, one way or another. He knows any who are there will have no idea who Tommy is, or that he shared breakfast with him most days. He wondered if they knew that Joe spent his time asking questions about life away from Blackpool, that he saw Slough as exotic, another world where the winds weren't cold and the sun shone with warmth. But Joe did love the off-season. He loved that Blackpool became his again, the pavements empty, a quietness, and he could get a pint in the pub without being heckled by stags and draped over by hens. Joe was a warmth for Tommy, and he deserves a proper send-off, no matter what his dad says.

The two of them stop, their arms hanging by their sides and they scan the long beach.

Must be a travelling fair, Dad? Don't you think?

Aye, must be. But they usually come with all sorts of wagons and I haven't ever seen a setup like this. In winter

Tommy looks ahead, down the long and winding promenade, beyond Central Pier, and sees stall after stall now erected, reds and whites like candy canes, yellows so bright it almost looks like the sun is out, bright blues like a clear sky. All appearing like they might have always been there.

No. Me, either. Maybe this is all a dream and really we're tucked up in bed?

His dad laughs and when Tommy looks he sees it is genuine.

If only, Son

We can go if you want

Al shakes his head, points his finger forward, and they press on, cutting themselves loose from the crowd to skim the edges.

You've changed your tune, Dad

Intrigued, Son. He glances at him as they walk. *Not every day you see a sight like this. Might never see it again*

They pass a group handing out buckets and spades freely, and grown men taking them.

For the kids? Tommy says, looking around, but children are scarce, only a few hanging onto their mothers' hands. He watches as the men plunge their spades into the wet sand and flick it into the buckets. Tommy laughs but really he knows he is scowling. And as they walk, side by side, the sound of the Wurlitzer rises above the din, above the howl of the wind, the tune instantly recognisable – 'I Do Like to Be Beside the Seaside' – and then beside him, his dad hums, *Oh! I do like to be beside the sea...* Tommy lifts onto his tiptoes, searching for the famous Tower Ballroom Wurlitzer, but only sees speakers, nothing genuine. A recording, and he realises it is on repeat – *Tiddely-om-pom-pom*. But all the same, he begins humming it, too, and they pass a rifle range. An elderly woman who is barely upright screeches as she hits the target and the grinning man thrusts a giant teddy bear at her. She hugs it tight, turning to nobody in her celebration. They keep walking.

I feel like we've woken up in a parallel universe, Dad

Same

But he sees his dad's shoulders loosen, the tightness around his jaw slacken as he watches the people – locals and visitors, alike – make their way to each stall, to each activity, to each entertainer. A woman brushes past them and leaves behind the sickly-sweet smell of candyfloss. His dad looks around.

Where's that from?

Over there, Tommy points to the child swirling the candyfloss around the stick like he'd done it a million times. The queue is long but he doesn't seem phased.

And Tommy sees the boy is taking no money, simply handing sticks into waiting hands and off they stroll. Al has already made his way into the queue.

You want candyfloss?

Yeah, he shrugged, *why not?*

I've never seen you eat candyfloss

You never saw me as a kid, did you?

Was it even invented then?

His dad laughs, *Cheeky git*

And Tommy realises that he has never imagined his dad as a child. Even in photographs, he's never associated the child with the man he's always known. The life before him. So, he takes the candyfloss stick in his hand and pulls off a large chunk, stuffing it into his mouth. His dad copies him, and they laugh, walking again with the flow of the crowd, passing sad looking donkeys with heavy-set men waiting their turn.

Come on, let's find Alicia. In his chest there is a niggle, a flutter of worry that she may be lost, that he has let his concern for her lapse and neglected to ensure she is safe. Like being a father, he thinks, although he is sure he will never know. *Dad, did you ever lose me?*

Huh? Oh my gosh, yes, a few times. Mostly in supermarkets or shopping centres. You were very curious. Your mother ended up putting reins on you. He laughs.

Like a dog lead?

Yes, just like that

Heel, boy

We'd usually find you in the sweet aisle. Or a toyshop. Although, one time you did walk into a lingerie shop, we assume looking for Mum, and all the women laughed at me as I dragged you out quick sharp

The scene plays so clearly to him like it might be a real memory, and he knows he would have been laughing, not realising the danger.

Punch and Judy! Al shouts. *She'll be there, I'm sure*

They walk quicker now, pushing past lingerers, those annoying people who stroll so slowly yet have no care for the hold-up they cause. He looks at his watch – 11 a.m.

Half an hour, but he says it more to himself than anyone else. And as the crowd parts, the theatre comes fully into view. Tall, draped in red velvet, the wind swishing the fabric as Tommy looks at the coat now draped across his arm, no memory at all of removing it. His dad has done the same.

There she is, Al points to Alicia who sits cross-legged at the front of the audience, her neck craned so far back it looks unhuman. She is laughing wildly, like the laughing man in the machine on the pier. She even rocks back and forth like him. Tommy moves around the edge of the audience in line with Alicia. She doesn't look away from Punch falling from his wooden horse, and the whole crowd howls with laughter.

Alicia! Tommy shouts. There's no sign that she has heard him, so he creeps closer, crouching. *Alicia!* She glances at him but then turns back to the theatre and laughs again. Tommy is now beside her and the crowd are tutting. *Alicia, Joe's funeral is any minute. We need to leave. Where's David and Mark?*

Alicia turns her face to Tommy and says, *Be away with ya, Tommy. Leave me be*

You don't want to come?

No, I don't

But it's Joe

Leave me be

He reaches his hand to her arm but she bats him away, her wrinkled, bony hand hitting much harder than he thought possible, and before he has time to stand and leave, she reaches her face to his and snarls, a low growl escaping her lips.

Jesus. Tommy stands and backs away, but she's no longer looking at him. She is back watching the show, her grin wide, her laugh loud, she rocks back and forth again.

What the hell happened there? Al says.

Alicia is very adamant she doesn't want to leave. And where the hell are David and Mark? I can't believe they've left her. He scans the crowd but really all he can think of is Alicia's evil stare, the dog-like growl, a side of her he has never seen before.

David and Mark are on the makeshift ballroom floor over there, waltzing

Tommy looks to where his dad is pointing and sees the floor, a glitter ball hanging from a pole, and a mash of bodies all circling in rhythm to the music.

Oh my God

Tommy surges forward and pulls at David's arm as he whizzes past him. David stops, open-mouthed and Mark keeps spinning for a moment, partnerless.

Why have you left Alicia?

Well, hello to you, too, Tommy. And we haven't left her. We know where she is and doubt very much she'll leave. She's glued to it

She's vulnerable

She's also not our problem, Tommy. Mark has joined them.

No, she's not, but you said you'd watch her

We have been. And now we're dancing

And very good we are, too. Mark eyes David and smiles. David strokes Mark's cheek and pouts his lips.

We really are, darling

Tommy has the urge to leave, to not watch these two fawning over each other. He looks at Al, who has turned his head away.

Can you please keep a check on her? Joe's funeral is any minute now. We should be leaving. I need to find George and Sheila

Oh, I think we'll give it a miss, to be honest. Joe would understand

You're not going, either?

No

David takes Mark's hand and twirls him.

Seriously?

They both stop and face Tommy.

Seriously! Now, with all due respect, please do fuck off

Tommy inhales, and Mark impersonates him, throwing the back of his hand to his forehead. But then they both turn and join the circling dancers once more.

In a Hole

The words repeat over and over, a tone Tommy has never heard from either of them, a look in David's eyes as he stares him down. His breakfast companions for nearly five years, now suddenly strangers.

Let's not pay any mind to them two. They're a strange pair, bicker like children, clearly haven't grown up enough themselves. Far too selfish for their own good

But Tommy doesn't agree. He sees David as a very caring type. The one he would most trust to watch over Alicia.

Alicia.

Dad, can we hurry up now? I don't want to leave her sat there much longer and risk losing her in this lot. She's so little and unsteady, this lot would swallow her up, trample her like a discarded sweet wrapper

His swinging arm hits a person on the back and it's then he notices the sheer number of people on the beach, like a million bees swarming in all directions, a buzz in their collective sound, and likely a sting if he catches that person with his arm again. He shifts around, hunching his shoulders to make his own body smaller.

Dad!

Al is being carried away, his head bobbing, and momentarily disappearing. Tommy pushes his way through the bodies, the stench of alcohol now strong as many swig bottles of beer and cider as they walk.

Fuck me, is this an England game or something? he says, and the woman beside him gives him a hard stare before thrusting her cider bottle into his mouth. The glass clashes with his teeth and he shouts at her but she's already pulled it away, swigging it down like pop. He wipes hard at his lips and looks down at her dirty hands, up at her sweaty face, and then gags, wiping even harder at his mouth. He moves as fast as he can away from her.

And then a hand grabs his arm and yanks him from the throng, out into clear air and he can breathe again, the stench of alcohol breath leaves with the crowd.

Dad, this is hell. Who are all these bloody people?

Couldn't say, Son. Maybe there's some kind of silent siren drawing them in, like some weird episode of Doctor Who, or something. He laughs.

So, the Daleks are going to appear? Exterminate, Exterminate

Or the Weeping Angels

Tommy shudders and Al laughs again.

Just keep your eyes open and don't blink

Dad!

Do you know your mother watched that episode from behind her fingers?

Did she?

She did. She was a big old scaredy cat

Nah. Not Ma. Nothing frightened her

Oh, you'd be surprised

Like what?

Silly things, mostly. Stuff we could laugh at. Did you know she thought our place was haunted?

No

Oh, yes. A poltergeist is what she thought. I just never told her it was mostly me leaving cupboard doors open or forgetting to lock the back door back up

Dad. What else?

Every sound in the night was a burglar. But she'd always be the one to check, so not really that scared, hey?

Imagine what would have been left of them if she'd found anyone

Ha! Not much, I'd say

The two are walking, ambling along the sea wall, safe, yards from the crowd. When Tommy looks again at the people, he sees a young boy swigging cider and wonders if it's the woman's. He shakes his head.

Animals, this lot

Ah, just having fun. Maybe they were desperate for it. Al stops and points to a tent up ahead. *Here, do you still have that twenty from Pat?*

Yeah, why?

Fortune teller, and he grins.

Are you serious? You want your fortune telling by a fraud in a head scarf?

No, I want to get away from this lot out here, and she's the only one with a tent. But Tommy hears something more in his voice, a curiosity.

Al presses on and pulls open the red curtain, ducking inside.

You're free? he says, as Tommy follows him inside.

The woman, her mouth turned down, her hair tousled in an undeliberate way, nods but says nothing. She instead holds out her hand. Tommy pulls the twenty from his pocket, placing it on the circular table before them. The woman drops her hand on the note and slides it inside her deep purple cloak, keeping her eyes on Tommy.

Sit, she says.

In the centre of the table is the crystal ball and around the tent, incense sticks burn, so many, they catch in Tommy's throat. There is a stench of damp, of un-washed, overused fabrics, likely stored in cold contain-ers that reminds him of his dad's attic. He has the urge to laugh but her eyes tell him that would not be wise.

Are you a travelling fair, or something?

She flicks her cheek with her tongue. *Or something,* she says.

His dad glances at him before looking back at her, and Tommy feels the same draw to not look away from her.

You have anything specific you like to know? Her ac-cent is thick, her voice deep, and her bushy eyebrows shield dark brown eyes.

Tommy shakes his head. *Just what the future holds For both of you, together?*

Tommy and Al look at each other and nod, and Tommy feels a warmth he has not felt for years, and he doesn't want to look away.

Father and son? she says, flicking her fingers from one to the other.

Yes, Tommy says.

Sweet. She closes her eyes and reaches her hands out to the ball. Her long fingers, wrinkled at the knuckles, swish and sway millimetres from the glass. Hypnotic-like. They seem to caress, her hands sensual, and then the noise from her throat, gentle, breathy. Tommy swallows, his eyes flicking from her hands to her face and back again. And when he looks back up, her eyes are open and on him, and he is sure he has been caught in an erotic thought. He feels his cheeks burn and lowers his head, but not before seeing the curl of her lips forming into a soft smile. His dad shifts in the seat next to him.

Time is short, she says. *There is not much future to see*

Not much? His dad says. *How much?*

She shrugs. *I cannot tell. But time is short for us all, yes?*

Yes, I suppose so. For some more than others

His dad's voice is heavy now.

Tommy's stomach knots.

Big changes coming, she says, and looks Tommy square in the eye.

For me?

For both. Resist the tide

What does that mean?

Resist the tide. I only pass what I can see

This is bollocks. So, Dad's going to die soon, and that's the big change coming? Thanks very much. I don't think I needed a crystal ball for that

Calm down, Son

I don't see death. I just see short time, she continues. *What you do with that short time is up to you. But change is coming and what you do with that is up to you*

And resist the tide?

She shrugs.

Great

She gestures with her hand towards the sea outside.

Resist the LITERAL tide? He hears his voice rising. *Dad, let's go*

Tommy stands but his dad is watching the woman, waiting for more.

I hear you, he says to her.

Thank you, she clasps her hands together and lowers her head.

Please, go happily on your way, she points to the opening, which Tommy is already halfway through. He glances back at her.

Big changes, she says again. *And mind the water. It's chilly this time of year*

He lets the canvas fall behind him to the sound of her chuckling inside.

Twenty pounds for that bollocks! But his skin has prickled.

His dad follows him slowly, and when he looks he sees a lightness in his face, a relief.

You're not taking that seriously? There's nothing wrong with you, Dad. You've years left

She didn't say I was going to die, Son. She's telling us to make the most of it, while we still can

And how does that fit with your Swedish clearance technique, cleansing yourself of everything?

His dad pauses. *It fits well, I think*

Well, I'm happy for you. Tommy throws his hands to his hips, looks away.

Yes, you sound it

Too much death, Dad. Too much. Mum, friends, Joe, my wife... He trails off.

Your wife didn't die

No. But the relationship did

All for the best, by all accounts

Al has shoved his hands into his pockets and is clenching his jaw.

Wait. You knew?

That you were married to a narcissist? Of course. Did you think me and your mother sat in silence? She was very worried about you. We both were

But you never said a word

Your mother said it for the both of us. You didn't need two people pecking at you

In his throat he feels the usual tightness.

I always knew you'd do what was best. You weren't raised to put up with shit like that

Tommy opens his mouth to reply, although he isn't sure what words, if any, might come out. But then his dad points to the sand below them, to a group of yelping adults.

Is that Sheila?

Tommy looks and sees her bending forward, clapping, shouting, a ridiculous expression on her face that looks almost vicious.

Sheila! Tommy shouts, but she doesn't look away from what's at her feet. Tommy moves closer and he can hear her screams now, like she's at the races about to win or lose a grand. She is clapping manically.

Tommy pushes through some cheering people and finds George in a hole, flinging sand with his hands like a dog digging. He is so deep, only his head is visible. And next to him is another hole, another man. A race.

What in God's name are they doing? Al has appeared next to him.

Racing. Digging, Tommy says, perplexed.

Racing to what? The Earth's core? Australia?

He can hear the laughter in his dad's words, the same incredulity.

Not a clue, Dad. Everyone's lost their minds

George! His dad shouts. *George, do you understand the physics of sand? Sand collapses at thirty-three degrees! You need to stop, George!* He moves to Sheila, grabbing her elbow, but she shoves him off. *Sheila, the sand will collapse on him. You need to stop him*

But Tommy watches as Sheila snarls at his dad, baring teeth, a deep growl, before a burst of laughter, spittle and all, lands in Al's face. His dad wipes frantically at his lips.

You animal!

Tommy launches towards his dad, skirting the edge of the hole and setting off an avalanche of sand. He doesn't look down, he keeps his eyes on his dad who is red with rage and about to flatten Sheila. He takes his arm and drags him away. Sheila turns back to the hole and starts yelling her encouragement again, screaming like a banshee, clapping wildly. But father and son leave them to their madness, pushing away, back towards the sea wall, to the comfort of space and relative quietness.

Can we go now? Al whispers.

*Yeah, I think so. And Joe's...*but Tommy goes to lift his shirt sleeve before realising he's already rolled it to the elbow. *Where's our coats?*

His dad claps his hands to his chest and looks around. *No idea*

In the fortune teller's tent?

No. I'm sure we were without them already, now I think about it

But it's freezing out here

Is it, though?

Tommy stands still, allowing the wind to wash over his bare skin. *No.* He blinks repeatedly. *Except it is. Isn't it?*

Looking around him, at the manic adults, the young children, so similar now he can't tell them apart, they are all almost bare-skinned, some in swimming trunks, some in bathing costumes, most in vests and shorts. All have hair whipping around their faces, sodden with winter drizzle.

With a sudden urge to leave, a chill in his bones if not in his skin, Tommy steps back.

Let's go, he swallows.

Go where?

Home? To yours? Nice cup of tea

Yes

But as they place their feet onto the huge sweeping steps that lead to the promenade, behind them they hear shouts, urgent screams, and Tommy looks over his shoulder to see a surge of people, like a wild pack of dogs lunging for their dying prey, a circle of limbs, a guttural call, Sheila's high-pitched cry, and they realise the centre of the melee is where George was.

It's All a Circus

DAD, LET'S LEAVE IT, hey? Tommy's body shakes, but he can't tell if it is fear, or an adrenaline telling him to run. He's always wondered if he would fight or take flight, and his urge to leave gives him the answer.

Has it collapsed?

Don't know. But there's a ton of people there. We'll only be in the way. You warned them

His dad turns to him, his eyes wide before they narrow. *Quite cold of you, that*

Yes, is all he can say. But his feet want to move as far from this group of people as possible. Home, to the familiar. The building dread inside of him now something he feels he could touch.

From the promenade walks the man in the top hat and red coat, a ringmaster, the hat stretching his frame beyond the ridiculous. He is a tower, and he worms his way through the people. Tommy watches his face closely, the harshness that is suddenly replaced by swift laughter, and then back to head teacher-like. Like a Jekyll and Hyde, he thinks. A deliberate attempt to be jovial. The man looks disgusted but then grins widely and pushes a bystander towards the crowd. They trip, lurch forward, turn to confront, and then laugh themselves. Reminiscent of mosh pits in his teens. In fact, as he scans the huddle, he sees many similarities – the drunkenness, the loudness, the body-to-body, sweaty armpit mass.

The top hat man turns and catches Tommy and Al in his sight. A full head above everyone else, he pouts his lips as if to say, *Don't you want to play?*, a tip of the head that makes the hat shift slightly. Tommy takes a step back but the railings jab his back. The man is approaching.

Let's go, Dad. He takes Al's arm and pulls him along the railings. As Tommy looks back over his shoulder, the man has stopped walking but is grinning, watching the two men leave.

Wonderful day for a fair, don't you agree? he shouts across the sandy expanse, his arms now lifted in the air. Around him people laugh and nod, speak their agreement, and the man turns, taking large strides as he pats individuals hard on the back. He pays no attention to the panicked cries from the holes, instead he strolls the opposite way and Tommy and Al round a bend, out of sight.

The pair walk in silence, side by side. Al has crossed his arms across his body, his face solemn, but he doesn't look back. Tommy falls into step with him, and notices for the first time that his dad is smaller, his body stooped yet also thinner. Never a big man, but always broad-shouldered, strong looking. Now the bulk is gone, the bones of his shoulders clear through his t-shirt.

Dad, where's your jumper?

My what?

Your wool jumper? You had it on a minute ago

His dad stops, puts his hand to his chin. *Oh, sure I did. I don't remember taking it off*

They look back along the railings but see nothing.

Do you want to go back?

I really don't

He frames his statement more as a question, a perplexed look in his eyes.

Are you cold?

No

And neither is Tommy, yet the winds are still there when he makes the attempt to notice them. He looks out at the Irish Sea, the brown churn of the Blackpool waters, the white foam of the crashing waves. Central Pier is now way back in the distance, North Pier much closer. The tide creeps ever so quietly away from them, but really the crash of the waters is drowned by the rowdy crowd, and if he focusses hard enough, he can hear the rhythmic calls of the waves, the splashes, he can see the spray. The winter waters as vicious as they always are.

The promenade is emptying of people as they descend more and more onto the sands, the water making way for them, as Tommy wonders how many more will come.

Have you seen Pat? Tommy says.

Likely back in the café by now, I'd say

Likely

He glances around, wondering if he will catch a glimpse of his Yankees baseball cap, but sees nothing, only strangers. The stacked-up deckchairs are now landing on the sand, blue and red stripes, rows of them, all looking out to sea. He sees people collapse like they've been on their feet all day. He looks at his watch. Noon.

My God, Dad, where's the time gone? It's lunch time

Never?

Tommy holds his wrist out to prove he isn't lying.

Nearly time to eat again

I'm still digesting my bacon, Dad

I guess Joe's thing will be nearly over now

And Tommy remembers the plan he had when he woke this morning, to eat breakfast with his dad, chat over the newspapers, catch up with the usual rabble, and say farewell to Joe. The pub beckoning in the afternoon, the bacon soaking up the beer. He isn't sure he's ever had plans go so far awry.

North Pier looms above them now, the old metal posts still wet with the morning tide, the criss-cross of girders holding it all up. And from atop the wooden planks, they hear numerous footsteps, some fast and playful, others slow and meandering. Here, at this end of the beach, is a peacefulness and the two men take deep breaths. He feels his dad move closer to him, almost shoulder to shoulder.

Let's catch our breaths, hey? he says.

Shall we sit?

The sand is still damp but his dad sits anyway, and Tommy drops next to him with a puff.

Resist the tide

He feels his dad's eyes on him, waiting for more of his thought to materialise, but nothing comes, not quickly anyway.

Yes. Good advice for life, don't you think?

In what way?

Well, you don't want a life that you simply get carried away on, do you? Who really wants that? It's what most of us get, mind you. The same thing day in and day out. It being all about earning enough to keep a roof over your head, or food on the table. Existing

Or like me, taking handouts to keep the roof over my head and put food on my table. Is that what you mean?

No. I mean both. Neither are truly living, are they?

Tommy takes a deep breath.

Do you think I'm a failure, Dad?

His dad doesn't answer straight away, instead he re-arranges his shoelaces before sitting more upright.

Failure, no. Do I think you've made some bad choices, got lost along the way? Yes, I do. But haven't we all?

Tommy's stomach drops at the judgement that has so easily fallen from his dad's tongue. He knows his ma would never have said such a thing to him.

He also tries to envision what mistakes his dad has made. He's always lived within his means, being a loving and supportive husband and father, owned his own house years ago, and still has all his own hair and teeth. A proper grown up.

He wants to rebut him, to throw something back, but he feels his throat tightening and can't trust the sound his voice will make.

Anyway, let's not dwell. Still plenty of choices coming your way

Al pushes himself up, still flexible in the hips and knees in a way that surprises Tommy.

What's that? His dad points under the pier into its shadow.

Don't know. Tommy shields his eyes as if this might make it clearer before realising the day is dull. He stands and moves a few steps closer. *Looks like a circus ring. There's a sad looking clown sat on the edge.* Tommy laughs.

A clown? His dad walks past him, his eyes trained on the dreary looking ring. When Tommy catches up with him, he sees an alertness, a pricking of his ears like a dog.

You like clowns? Tommy laughs again, wondering at this sprightliness beside him.

Tommy, I love clowns

His words are so matter of fact, as if to say, *How do you not know that?*

Sorry, I had no idea. Do you want to say hello?

I do

They move quickly and his dad stops in front of the clown, a wide grin on his face. But he doesn't speak to him. He takes him in, walking from side to side. The clown keeps his head down, pretending he doesn't know they are there even though they are impossible to miss. His dad stretches his fingers towards the clown's face.

Wonderful makeup. Such a sad face. Look at that acting, Tommy. Isn't it fabulous?

Is he acting, or is he actually sad? It's been a weird day

Of course it's acting! He's in character. This is the lovesick Pierrot pining over his lost love, Columbine

And with that, the clown raises his head, his white face, the red dot at the end of his long nose, and the black tear-like streaks that fall from his eyes. He looks at Al and Al looks at him and tips his head.

I could be Harlequin? he says to the clown, and with that the clown stands and balls his fist.

Dad

It's fine, Son. Harlequin is his arch enemy, the true love of Columbine. Do you want me to be Harlequin? he asks the clown.

The clown lowers his head, his shoulders drooping, and he gives a resigned nod, an acceptance that he will never be rid of him anyway.

Marvellous! His dad is smiling widely, moving to the back of the ring, pulling out the costumes. Manic in a way that makes Tommy's heart race as he looks around, praying that nobody is watching as his dad crawls around on his hands and knees. And the thought occurs to him that regression is a sign of dementia but then berates himself for letting his mind go there so easily.

Dad, we don't have time for this. But Pierrot lurches forward, wagging his finger in Tommy's face, his frown now a scowl. Tommy takes a step away.

His dad is buried in the pile of costumes, pulling items out, discarding the ones that aren't right. A man slightly possessed. Yet, also, a man who knows what it is he is looking for.

Dad?

Found it! And he pulls from the mass of fabrics a red and black outfit that to Tommy looks like a tent. *Help me out here*

Al is already stepping into the costume, pushing his feet through the bulbous legs, one red, one black. He shimmies his body into the rest of it until he is covered to the neck. *Do up the back for me, Son*

Dad, come on!

Please, Son! Just zip it up

Tommy steps into the ring, over to the animated bulk of his father, and he wants to laugh at the ridiculousness of him but knows not to. He slides the zip up to his neck.

Al spins to Pierrot and holds his arms out as if to say, *Will this do?*

But Pierrot throws his hand up, crosses his arms and turns away.

No, he's right. We are only half done. Tommy, grab the white face paint

Dad, I'm not putting makeup on you

Yes, you are. And it's not makeup. It's face paint. It's the character

He picks up the tray and the sponge and holds it out to Tommy.

Dad, I don't understand what's happening here, he says, taking the tray and lathering the sponge in the white, clay-like substance.

Making your old dad happy, Son. That's all

But clowns?

His dad closes his eyes and Tommy smears the face paint over his wrinkled skin, having to massage it in around the crow's feet of his eyes and the deeper-set lines of his forehead. Within minutes, his face is a white mass, ghost-like, and his grey eyes blink out at him.

Now, black diamonds around the eyes

How do you know all of this?

Tommy looks at Pierrot, who is shifting closer, glancing and then looking away, shaking his head, sulking.

He draws the diamonds and colours them black, before Al grabs the red and carefully paints his own lips.

Nearly there, he says. And from the pile next to him, he pulls a head-dress, horn-like, one red, one black, and they droop at the ends. His dad, transformed.

Pierrot stands. He holds his arms out to his companion, melancholy on his face. The two approach each other, they side-step, they reach out but miss. And Tommy laughs as Pierrot becomes annoyed at his friend, his dad so light on his feet as if he is twenty again. Pierrot extends his arms in a hug, and as he closes them, Harlequin moves and Pierrot tumbles to the floor. Harlequin puts his hands on his hips and shakes his head. Will Pierrot never learn?

And as the two continue their game of cat and mouse, Tommy begins rummaging through the pile of discarded clown remnants, not knowing what goes with what, but gathering the things he is attracted to. Bright reds, blues, curly-haired wigs. Traditional. And he finds himself laughing wildly to himself, while in the background Pierrot and Harlequin battle, and in the distance the sea roars and the people yell louder and louder until their voices become the sea.

We're All Clowns Here

On the end of Tommy's nose sits a red, fluffy ball, on his head a fuzzy red and blue wig. His clown shoes are about a size fourteen, and he trips when he walks. But he finds the comedy of his body comes naturally. The oversized movements, the intentional slips, the voice that comes as if it is from another.

And here, ladies and gentlemen, we have the oldest and closest of friends, driven apart by their love of the same maiden, finally reunited! Tommy shouts to the invisible crowd.

Pierrot and Harlequin have managed to embrace, and the brief love turns quickly to hate. Tommy circles them and when Pierrot shoves Harlequin and he stumbles backwards, Tommy allows him to fall into him, to tumble dramatically to the floor. The two now a heap. Pierrot points and throws his head back in silent laughter.

Tommy and Harlequin wrap their limbs around each other, both men attempting to stand, and Tommy finds himself copying his dad, watching his very deliberate moves, until the two of them are moving in unison. Tommy releases himself and leaps to his feet, his hands on his hips.

Now then, do watch out for innocent bystanders! And Harlequin bows in apology and Pierrot flicks his hand in disgust. Tommy dusts himself down and knocks his red nose to the floor. He picks it up and puts the nose in his open mouth, then onto his eye, screwing his eyelids to hold it in place. Behind him, the laughter of a child. Tommy turns to see a young boy, elbows on the edge of the circus ring, a wide grin on his face.

An audience.

Pierrot and Harlequin spot him too, and Pierrot steps towards him with a wild wave. But Harlequin side-steps and shoves him out of the way, bowing deeply before he gets a boot to his rear end and face plants the floor. The boy laughs hysterically, and Pierrot smiles with jazz hands.

Tommy takes a step away, leaving the two to battle it out for the attention of the boy, and he can see why they fell for the same woman. He looks over his shoulder back along the beach, the quietness a relief as he takes some deep breaths. The crowd is still there, now black ants milling back and forth, the sounds just distant muffled rumbles, the occasional high-pitched shriek as the wind blows their voices their way.

Turning back, he watches. The stiff father he is so used to, seemingly now so agile. A man reborn before him. His dad's happiness seems catching as Tommy finds himself grinning, a warm churning in his stomach. From behind him comes splashes but when he looks he can see nothing. A wave, he thinks.

Al is now sitting on the edge of the ring, catching his breath. The young boy is pulling at his costume, flicking the ends of Harlequin's headdress. His dad ducks and weaves, first laughing, before the boy pulls the headdress from his head, and his father grabs the boy by the arms, shaking him.

Dad, easy. Tommy walks over to them and leads the boy away.

No manners! Just like the rest of that rabble out there

Pierrot is sulking in the background and Tommy can't tell if he is acting or not. He takes a seat next to his dad.

Shall we get going?

No

No?

I'm not going back to that lot

His dad is looking back down the beach, and Tommy sees the man in the top hat weaving through them. He notices again the forceful way he is shoving some of them, playful, laughing, pointing out at the water.

We don't have to go back that way. We could head home and get that cup of tea we talked about

Not yet. We can't leave Pierrot alone

Pierrot has reached his arms out straight and is tugging at the black gloves on his long fingers, straightening them. He is flattening his ruffles on his costume, straightening his tattered edges.

He thinks she is coming, that if he waits long enough, pines hard enough, he will be rewarded

Columbine?

Of course, Columbine

But it's fictional?

His dad sighs.

Do you not think that the man beneath the costume is always Pierrot? In some way or other? He has taken that man inside himself, he has become him

But it's a costume, Dad

Shaking his head he says, *No. You are wrong. He is a nobody beneath that. He is likely old, lonely. Until he is who he is supposed to be. Pierrot. Well-known throughout the world, heartbroken, longing.* Al looks Tommy up and down. *Who are you?*

Tommy

Al throws his hands in the air. *You don't even know who you have become! You are Auguste!*

Who the hell is Auguste, and how do you know all of this this?

Stand up, his dad says. *Put your nose back on*

Tommy pushes the bright red ball onto his nose and Al drags him back into the centre of the ring.

Here we have Pierrot. He gestures towards the white-faced clown, slumped with his chin in his hand. *The intelligent, guiding figure of our world. A leader. That was until I, Harlequin, came along. I outwitted him, drove him to distraction, and became the romantic lead*

You stole his love

She was never his to steal

Dad

Harlequin!

I can't call you that

His dad takes steps away from Tommy, into the centre of the ring. Tommy looks around him, at the people lingering in the shadows, further under the pier where the day is even duller. They are all topless, he notices now. His skin bumps at the thought of it.

And now, in an attempt to lighten the mood of our esteemed Pierrot, Auguste arrives! Al sweeps his hand in a way that tells Tommy to follow him. He steps into the ring, now entirely conscious of his body and the ridiculous costume that drapes from it. *He brings with him a comedy of errors, a slapstick hilarity, a loving disposition*

Loving?

Yes. You are kind

I am kind

Too kind

Al tips his head, and for a moment he is not Harlequin, at least not in his eyes.

You are the light to Pierrot's dark, his dad continues. Tommy pulls a red silk from his sleeve, and keeps pulling as it turns blue, pink, orange, yellow. Pierrot has stood now, his hand across his mouth, watching him, a smile forming behind his fingers. *You are the bringer of happiness*

His dad looks at him again, a strangeness to his face, to the way he his holding his gaze.

Are you trying to say something, Dad?

Harlequin! He yells with a spit.

Am I not the 'bringer of happiness'?

Of course not, Tommy! You have brought only your sadness. Stay in character, for fuck's sake!

But I was sad! I am sad!

Yes. So was I. But I no longer want to be, yet you are keeping me there, in that dark place

Tommy drops the silks to the dirty floor and Pierrot scoops them up, running them through his fingers, watching the two intently.

Al turns away, shakes his shoulders over and over like an athlete might.

Do you know I used to be able to do the Harlequin flips, the cartwheels, the somersaults?

No! How would I know that when you have never told me?

Maybe it's the case that you never listened to me. Only to your mother

Are you going to somersault now? Tommy laughs.

Of course not, you moron!

Fucking hell, Tommy looks at Pierrot who has turned his mouth down, widened his eyes, turned his palms upwards in silent question. *I don't know, Pierrot. I really don't*

And Pierrot sits cross-legged on the floor, pulling Auguste down with him. They sit facing each other and Tommy wants to look anywhere other than in his sad eyes. Pierrot reaches out and quickly swipes the nose form Auguste's face.

Hey! He grabs for it, but Pierrot squeezes it tight in his fist. He holds out both hands, his fists still clenched. He nods to each and Tommy taps the one he knows the nose is in. But Pierrot opens his hand with a flourish and it is empty. Tommy laughs and taps the other, but it is also empty.

What? But where? Tommy looks around him and Pierrot opens his mouth wide in a grin and the red furry ball drops from his lips. Tommy laughs.

See? his dad says from the side of the ring. *Laughter*, and Tommy sees he is smiling in a sad way. *You forget what it's like when you have nobody to laugh with*

Tommy's shoulders drop and he pushes himself up. He takes a breath, wobbles his head and un-straightens his tie, wiggling his fingers, his eyes on his dad. He takes a step forward, but rocks back again, one step forward, two steps back. He stops. Wiggles his tie. Walks forward again, staggers sideways. His dad giggles. Auguste looks at the floor as if it is to blame. He puts his foot forward again and trips, rolling into a ball on the ground. He looks up, sheepishly, hoping nobody saw, then wipes his brow in relief. Harlequin is now shaking his head in disbelief at Auguste's clumsiness. He holds his hand out to pull him up, but as Auguste reaches for him, Harlequin snatches it away, touches his thumb to his nose and sticks out his tongue. Now Pierrot is silently belly laughing. Harlequin stands with his back stiff, his legs straight and his hands on his hips. He raises his chin, and suddenly he is debonair, almost royal.

It is in this manner that they proceed, the three of them circling each other, interacting with simple mime and wild expression. Tommy becomes Auguste, Al falls willingly into the clutches of Harlequin, and Pierrot is always Pierrot. Auguste brings laughter, Harlequin wit and cunning, Pierrot veers wildly from ecstasy to melancholy. But they are three. They are the embodiment of sadness, happiness, camaraderie, and the afternoon passes around them. No audience presents itself, only the fleeting, topless, trouserless, pasty-white body of a person running past the ring. Still, screams brush them from afar, but only Pierrot glances into the distance, back down the beach, out to sea.

Auguste and Harlequin bond. Harlequin teaching Auguste the ways of the clown, because there is nobody more clownish than Auguste. He berates him when he falls short of a laugh, kicks him gently on the rear to show affection, and the two grin regularly at each other, sometimes remembering that they are Al and Tommy, father and son, and that they have never laughed this much in each other's company before.

But around them the day is dying. The winter hours are drawing in, and the tide is returning. Al's Harlequin loses his debonair quality, his upright shoulders, and he slumps into a mild panic, his eyes wide, his mouth slightly open. Pierrot is pushing props and costumes into the over-sized sacks. Pierrot is peeling off parts of his own being, becoming somebody else in front of Harlequin's eyes.

Dad, you ok?

Al doesn't reply, instead he swallows.

Come on, Dad, it was just a little fun. And the tide is heading back in. We'll be swamped soon

Tommy takes off his nose and looks out to where the water is breaking against the pier. He sees a shape, but it is grey against a murky brown and then it is gone. A dirty sea throwing up its junk. He moves towards his dad, his arm outstretched.

Come on, time to head home I think

His dad takes a step backwards.

Dad, don't be ridiculous

I'm not going, he says, his voice wavering.

Tommy laughs. *Of course you're going. Pierrot is going. The whole ridiculous lot of them are going*

Tommy looks at Pierrot and he is glaring at him.

Sorry. I didn't mean you. It's been a long day

Pierrot shrugs and goes back to stuffing items into the sacks.

Al is shaking his head. He throws himself to the floor, crosses his legs and folds his arms. A protest. If shackles were available, he would attach himself.

Dad, this is embarrassing

I don't care

Pierrot stands and walks towards his dad. He reaches out and pulls at the headdress on Al's head but Al grabs it with both hands. The two enter a battle of sorts, a back-and-forth tug of war.

Now, come on, Tommy says. *No need to get physical, Pierrot. He's an old man*

But as Tommy lifts his leg to step back in the ring, a hand lands on his shoulder.

What's this?

Tommy looks up at the tall man in the top hat. His voice is deep, playful, yet stern. *Did mummy not teach you when play time is over?* He is speaking directly to Al but his hand remains on Tommy, and when he tries to move away, the fingers tighten.

Look, he's just enjoyed himself, that's all

I can speak for myself, Tommy. His dad stands up, snatching the headdress from Pierrot's fingers, and walks towards the top hat man. *This hasn't been play-time for me, Sir. It's been a realisation of a dream. Being a clown*

The man laughs. *We are all clowns here*

The two men look at each other for what feels like a long time. They are searching each other's faces, waiting for the other to break. Tommy can only stand there, his words not needed, not cared for. Eventually the man relaxes his shoulders, releases his tight grip on Tommy without entirely letting him go. From him comes a smell, sweet and sickly, like his ma on a baking day, all caster sugary and buttery, and Tommy might have filled his mouth with spare hundreds and thousands. This man in black and red, statuesque and long-fingered, has never baked in his life, and he wonders if maybe he is a child-eater.

You want to remain a clown? the man asks.

Tommy watches his dad's face closely, waiting for him to laugh and playfully wave him away. *Of course not*, he expects his words to be.

But instead comes a flat, emphatic *YES*.

Onwards

It is in this moment, in the silence that has fallen around the four men, that Tommy really sees his father for the first time. He watches as he animatedly speaks, attempts to convince, shows enthusiasms way beyond anything Tommy has ever seen before. He doesn't catch all his words, he doesn't need to. The father in front of him now is the most alive he has ever been.

He fights hard to find a memory from childhood, because there must be one where his father was filled with excitement. There must have been. Yet he can find none. Loving, yes. Kind, yes. A role model, yes. But excited? Even at Christmas, the only excited member of their house was Tommy. Even when his mother brought a puppy home, there were simple smiles, but nothing more.

The man in the top hat has taken a seat on the edge of the ring, finally releasing Tommy, and he is listening intently to Al.

Tommy takes a few steps away, looking back towards the dying crowd. The day has dimmed to almost nothing and the people have done the same. There are stragglers only, they stagger in the new quietness. And when he looks at the promenade, he sees it is also empty. Every stall, every activity packed away and gone. Even the deckchairs. Even the Wurlitzer on repeat has been silenced.

Where have they all gone? Tommy says to the man in the top hat, who turns to look at him, mid-sentence.

Packed up, gone home. Fun is over for today

But they were there not long ago

I think it was longer ago than you remember. The tide is almost returned

Tommy looks at the water, lapping close to the ring now.

Shit. We better get moving

We? the man says.

Well yes, us. We need to move. It will take the ring

The man laughs.

I'm not worried. He looks at Pierrot. *You are all packed?*

Apart from their costumes, yeah

It is the first time Tommy has heard his voice. He is southern, his accent laced with the traits of a market trader, maybe a fish seller. Confident, a bit cheeky. Not Pierrot.

Gentlemen, the top hat man says, *can we now move along, let Pierrot roll up the ring. Keep the costumes for now*

I don't want mine, you can have it. Tommy pulls off his wig, his scalp itchy with relief.

Tommy! Wait. Please wait

His dad is scrambling out of the ring towards Tommy. He grabs him by the arm and leads him to the steps, away from the listening ears.

I'm so tired, Dad, I really just want to go home to bed

You have a lifetime to be tired

Where have they all gone?

Home. I can't do it, Tommy. I can't go back

Go back? Tommy looks at his dad, his eyes wet, his cheeks rosy with wind and life.

His dad stares out to sea, contemplating his next words.

I trained for years as a young lad with the Tower Circus, I was understudy to so many clowns. I learnt it all. The art of it, because it truly is an art

I never knew that, and in that moment he feels a betrayal, a hidden family secret, a part of him that he had never been given the privilege of knowing.

No. I haven't talked about it much. It's my biggest regret

What is?

Not fulfilling the dream, Tommy.

What stopped you?

His dad looks deep into Tommy's eyes. *Life. Responsibility*

You mean, I stopped you?

Not in the way you're saying it, no. But when babies come along, priorities change. Regular income is needed. Security. It was so seasonal. So, your mother and I decided it wasn't the right time. Only, the right time never came back around again

Tommy sighs and looks over at Pierrot/fish seller.

The ring master has said I can join them. We can join them

Tommy laughs. *You're kidding me, right? These people we've been running from all day?*

They take a bit of getting used to, like any travelling group. But we'll be taken care of, once you're in the circle

Dad, this is ridiculous

Looking out at the creeping tides, he says with a sadness, *I knew you'd say that*

Well of course I'm saying that! Because it is ridiculous. You want to pack up and leave with them

The afternoon air has turned, a shift in the direction of the wind, easterly, distinctly colder on their bare skin. Tommy looks around for his discarded clothing and finds none. A short-sleeved shirt in January. His dad is the same, and he sees goosebumps running up his arm, and has the urge to wrap him in something. But before he moves, his dad says, *I* am *leaving with them, Tommy*

Dad

If only to see. There's no harm, is there? Only opportunity. Only the chance to finally do it and see. To become Harlequin

Tommy opens his mouth to protest, but his dad's face is pleading, suddenly the child wanting sweets before his tea, and Tommy turns instead to the man in the ridiculously oversized hat, who makes his stomach knot and churn, his heart race a little faster. *What even are you?*

The man smiles and walks gently towards them, his fingers clasped in arrogance before him.

We are the Off-Season. He says with a nod, a sweep of his arms. *We bring smiles to the winter gloom. Who says everything has to die in winter? Who says it can't carry on, rain or shine?*

And you travel?

Of course. Seaside town to seaside town. A day, and then on we go

You make money?

This is a crude question to ask a stranger, he smiles.

You have permits?

So many questions

Tommy, stop it. You're being rude

Where have all the people gone?

We are not responsible for the visitors. His voice hisses on the end of the word. *They come, they go. We pay no attention to their greediness, the often vile behaviours like animals at times, thinking they are due a good time, a time to be childlike. That they take our candyfloss and doughnuts so willingly for free and drop their wrappers for others to pick up. All of that is fine. All we care about is the smiles. Because what is life without smiles?* And the man smiles widely, even his eyes, crow's feet trailing his modestly aged face. Teeth straight and white, his lips elongated, almost feminine.

You have definitely made me smile, Al says, and the man lowers his head in thanks. *And we dropped no litter*

Our people are also free to come and go as they please

See. I can try it and see, Tommy. No ties. Time is short, Son

My god, you're using her words now

The man moves away, checking on the progress of Pierrot and the dismantling of the ring.

Dad, please don't do this. I don't trust them

Son, I grew up with these people. Yes, they live differently to us. No, I probably won't enjoy their company for too long. But to be Harlequin alongside Pierrot, to draw a crowd and perform, it could be so fabulous. Even if just once

Tommy shakes his head. He sees the warmth now in his dad's eyes, the imaginings of his dream coming true. *I'm not going to convince you to stay, am I?*

No, Son. And I'd love it if you'd come with me. The troupe together

Tommy looks down at his clown feet.

I will never have this opportunity again. Make your old man happy

We leave soon, shouts the man, *we won't be waiting. Or can I convince you to take a dip? A swim in the warm waters of the Irish Sea? The true sign of a day at the beach, as you drag your weary bones and salty skin home.* The man laughs and Tommy looks at the sea, now a darkened mass before him, creeping closer and closer by the second, threatening to swallow his feet, the darkened sky mirroring the sea.

Pierrot walks over now, the sacks hanging over his shoulder.

Either come, or hand them back. He gestures at their costumes.

Tommy. His dad's voice is no longer pleading, more an order, his watery eyes now firm and focussed.

My God, Dad

His dad turns away from him, looks at Pierrot. *Count me in*, he says, and Pierrot simply shrugs and walks away, up the steps.

The time is now, the top hat man says. He sweeps his hand at Tommy, a now-or-never gesture.

Shit, Tommy whispers, watching his dad follow Pierrot.

He looks back down the beach, now completely empty. He looks out to sea, the dark water churning with darkened shadows. A dream. It feels a dream. He is sure if he was to wake now, his day would start again. Maybe he won't have missed Joe's funeral. Maybe Alicia will be sipping tea by the window, pulling card decks from her pocket. The same routine, day in, day out, still waiting to happen. Maybe town will remain empty of people, as it should be, because Blackpool in the off-season *is* a dull place, it *is* a miserable place, it *is* a cold place. As it should be.

But then he watches his dad up on the promenade, his steps quick, his body light, his voice nattering away to a smiling Pierrot. Comrade. Something Tommy has never been to him. *You only brought your sadness.* The top hat man is watching him quietly, waiting.

What does it mean to leave with you tonight? Is that not a strange thing to do?

He shrugs and smiles. *Not much stranger than staying put in a dead town. But you are simply dragging things out now, Sir. We know you won't leave your father alone in his adventure*

Adventure?

Of course! Life is, and should be, an adventure

But he is old

He doesn't seem old to me. Maybe it is you who is old. Old of mind

Tommy laughs because he knows he is right.

He can no longer remember his childhood dreams, although he must have had them. Everything got sucked up by her, the wife, like she turned his lights out one by one. And he let her.

His dad is now gesticulating to Pierrot and he hears a sharp laugh. And Tommy sees he has the power to be her in this moment. The one to turn his dad's light out.

Top hat man tips his head, his long fingers asking Tommy to lead the way. Tommy walks with long strides, the clown feet cumbersome, up the steps. His dad and Pierrot are waiting, his dad's grin wide, his eyes alive.

Son

Dad. Tommy leans into his ear. *We leave if it gets weird, ok? Any sign*

His dad taps his shoulder and nods. Tommy feels at his pockets beneath the costume, his wallet with cash, his phone that nobody ever rings.

An adventure, Tommy. A break, a reset. Something so different we can't possibly be bored. Something Joe might be proud of us for, that he might ask us questions about on our return

Tommy's throat tightens and he reaches his hand to his dad's.

You want me to come? You seem pretty set on it, with or without me

With you, obviously. But happy you, only. Please

And now Tommy remembers Alicia's face, so full of childish laughter, the way she had fought viciously to hold onto that moment. And David and Mark, waltzing like their relationship depended on it. Sheila and George happy in the only way they knew how to be – by winning. And was this it? Had the travellers succeeded? A light amid the long winter gloom?

Tommy, his dad and Pierrot stand by the curb. Top hat man sits on the wall of the promenade. He crosses his legs, his face serene, slightly tired, like most families after a long day at the beach. Bodies heavy with weariness, but hearts full. Memories made. Tommy wonders then where the little boy is from this morning and whether he is still being pestered for photographs. He imagines him in a diner sipping a chocolate milkshake and biting hard into a burger, his mum scrolling their memories. And Pat, likely back at the café, awaiting the next morning when he will be two short for breakfast. And Tommy feels a relief, a weight lifted from his shoulders. People he no longer has to placate with pleasantries. A father who might not glare at him over his mug of tea, the person he sees as keeping him sad. That being over makes Tommy smile and reach for his dad's elbow.

Alright, Son?

Yes, Dad

And from along the prom, the charabanc chugs. Black, large, bouncy.

Here we go, Tommy says.

Indeed, his dad smiles.

The bus pulls up and the driver squeezes the horn. Tommy and Al jump.

Now then, might we ever get used to that?

Unlikely, Dad. And Tommy looks to the driver who is pouting his lips triumphantly.

Tommy scans the bus, full to bulging. They sit in tired silence, watching the newcomers approach. There are small waves and Tommy hesitantly smiles back at them.

Is there room? he says to the top hat man.

Oh yes, always room

Pierrot climbs aboard and vanishes between bodies.

After you, Tommy takes his dad's hand and helps him up the steps.

Looking back out to the churning January seas, Tommy feels the usual chill in his bones. The tide is now fully in and in the murk of dusk, he still sees the roll of objects in the waves. There one second gone the next. A trick of the light. Detritus from the seabed. Seaweed wrapped around plastic. Pasty white, like the skin of a winter seasider. He glances along the promenade, not a single reminder that the travellers had ever been here. Not a single soul left wandering, as is right. Tommy turns and climbs the steps and when he looks back over his shoulder, he sees top hat man turn to the sea, scan the waters and take a deep bow.

Hurry along now, the driver shouts in Tommy's ear, his words mocking. *Time to move on*

Tommy takes the final step aboard the bus and sees dozens of eyes watching him. The young boy, now sickly looking from all the candyfloss. Many bare bodies, clad scantily in bikinis and briefs. The puppeteer who entertained sweet Alicia for hours. He keeps walking, stepping over feet.

To the back, the driver calls after him. So, Tommy pushes forward.

And on his wrist a hand. He looks down at the dark eyes of the fortune teller. She smiles in that knowing way of hers. *You resisted the tide*, she says. *As I knew you would*

Her words are playful, sexual even, although Tommy is never sure of these things. Her fingers linger on his wrist, a gentle stroke and as he walks away she holds on until he is out of reach. He is now very aware of his clown face, his clown feet, nothing really to be attracted to at all, and he shakes his head.

His dad is on the back row of the charabanc, a young woman to his left, sleeping, and an older man to his right. Tommy sits down between his dad and the sleeping woman. He sighs, realising his legs ache, his feet burn. In fact, his entire body hurts. Like the days he remembers from childhood. The long, hot days with friends, where he forgot to eat and returned home just before dark. And Tommy smiles. The feeling is a nice one in his bones.

The top hat man has now boarded and stands like a giant at the front.

Ladies and gentlemen, let us extend a warm Off-Season welcome to Al and Tommy, our new Harlequin and Auguste. A fine addition to a lonely Pierrot

The bus laughs gently and they all turn to wave at the clowns at the back of the bus.

Tommy lifts his hand, his dad shouts, *hello*, but Tommy wonders how the man knows their names.

Now, onwards! And the top hat man sits at the front alongside the driver. He takes off his hat to reveal jet black, curly hair. The driver honks the horn as he pulls away from the curb, and Al rests his head on Tommy's shoulder.

Tommy looks up at the tower, consumed at the top by misty cloud. On his face he feels the light fall of drizzle as the day had started. The Blackpool streets are mostly empty, straggler tourists heading for tea or to retire back to their B&B. Maybe George and Sheila's annual guest is regaling them in his antics for the day. He hopes so. He hopes he has more stories to tell than a trip to the pub on the corner.

Tommy turns to look out the back of the charabanc. At the sea, and the waves, and feels the relief in his chest to be leaving it behind, even if just for a while. He takes deep breaths of the cold, sea air. But there, on the top of the sea wall, he sees Alicia's bright pink coat folded neatly alongside Pat's Yankees baseball cap and apron. And more piles of clothes, all neatly folded, deliberate. Then David's red-spotted shirt with Mark's blue Paisley jacket, Sheila's woolly hat. Nothing of George's. Yet dozens and dozens of other's clothes, one pile after the other. Tommy looks again at the sea. The objects floating and churning. But before he can stand, to keep looking, to check, the bus turns right and the promenade, the sea, Blackpool, disappears.

Acknowledgements

First of all, I want to say a massive thank you to Ariell Cacciola for taking a chance on this unpublished writer, and for giving me the best first taste of publication I could have had. It's been wonderful.

To Curtis Brown and Alice Lutyens for their support and advice.

To all the amazing early readers who have given me fantastic blurbs and reviews, thank you!

To my brilliant writing tribe, particularly Jade Reilly, Sarah Lupton, Asha Hick, Jennifer Kennedy, Jennie Godfrey and my CBCWrite Inners. Writing would be so lonely without all of you.

To Katie and Carolyn at Storytellers, Inc, the best local bookshop, for championing me and stocking my book. This means the world.

To my family and friends, for always understanding how important this writing game is to me and supporting me in every way. Especially to my husband, Ben.

And finally, to Blackpool, my birthplace. Stay weird.

About the Author

Jodie Robins is a fiction writer based on the Fylde Coast in Lancashire. She is a graduate of the Curtis Brown Creative Novel Writing programme, and has since signed with Alice Lutyens at Curtis Brown. Her writing is influenced by anything dark and gothic, exploring themes around isolation, loss and grief, and family. Jodie is currently editing her debut novel with her agent.

About The Northern Weird Project

This book is a part of The Northern Weird Project by Wild Hunt Books, a collection of six pocket-sized novellas by authors who are writing and living in the North of England.

Incorporating eerie and uncanny incidents, these novellas investigate aspects of the North through setting, subject and character.

All books in this series are available to order from our bookshop.
https://www.wildhuntbooks.co.uk/bookshop

More From The Northern Weird Project

This House Isn't Haunted But We Are
by Stephen Howard

Simon and Priya's young daughter has died in a tragic accident. Determined to heal their fracturing marriage, the couple move to the North Yorkshire Moors to renovate a dilapidated rural cottage. However, they just can't process their grief as increasingly eerie events unfold. A child's ghostly figure appears on the moors, doors lock themselves, and a mysterious stain grows from the loft. Is it their daughter haunting them or something else?

(Don't) Call Mum
by Matt Wesolowski

Leo is just trying to catch his train back home to the village of Malacstone in North East England. But there's disorder at the station, and when a loud young man heading for London boards the train accidentally, a usually easy journey descends into darkness and chaos. The train soon breaks down in the middle of nowhere, and as night falls, something...or someone steps out of the distance. Is it a man or something far more sinister?

The Retreat
by Gemma Fairclough

Richard's sister Julie returns home from a mysterious wellness facility in remote Cumbria in 1994. He's convinced that this place was a cult and was the cause of his sister's eventual suicide. Finally, after years as an unaccomplished academic, he decides to investigate the disturbing accusations against the Hartman Retreat Centre. Then he meets Lucy, a young woman whose story is eerily similar to his sister's decades before. Richard is determined to unearth what's really been happening at the Hartman Retreat Centre but more importantly, who is Charles Hartman, the celebrated healer who casts a powerful hold over all who come to the retreat.

Good Boy

by Neil McRobert

After a boy vanishes on the outskirts of a small Northern town, a woman spies from her window a mysterious
man digging a grave in the exact spot of the disappear-
ance. However, when she confronts him, the man's true
purpose is far more chilling than she could have imagined and the history of the town's fatal past unfolds.
What has been hiding in this small northern town all
these years? A gripping story of supernatural horror,
nostalgia and mystery.

Turbine 34

by Katherine Clements

It's 2035 and England is experiencing the hottest summer in living memory. A 61-year-old environmental
scientist, is tasked with evaluating the impact of a con-
troversial new wind farm on the West Yorkshire moors.
Camped out alone at Turbine 34 which was built on
the ancient peat bog, she soon discovers signs of the
devastation caused by the construction, she begins to
see things that shouldn't be there. She has dedicated her
life to protecting the moor, but will it protect her?

Wild Hunt Books would like to thank the following Lifetime Supporters:

Daniel Sorabji

Jan Penovich

Blaise Cacciola

BECOME A SUPPORTER BY CONTACTING US AT

INFO@WILDHUNTBOOKS.CO.UK

The Publisher would also like to thank the following early supporters of The Northern Weird Project:

Aidan Smith

Alex Herod

Ali W

Alicia Lomas-Gross

Anthony Martin

Beth Baskett

Bethany Vare

Blair Rose

Carmen

Charlotte Platt

Charlotte Tierney

Emma Armshaw

Freya S

George Dunn

Heidi Marjamäki

Ianthe May

J. Aaron Courts CWO4, USMC, Retired

Jeff

Jennifer B. Lyday

K. Wicks

Kelsey Stoddard

Kirsty Logan

Laura Elliott

Lisa Elliott

Lynne G

Mandy Bublitz

Mark Taylor

Martyn Waites

Monica Voynovska

Nicola Leedham

Nina Woodcock

Rachel Bridgeman

Rosie Warfield

Samuel Best

Sheena E. Perez

Sonja Zimmermann

Sophy Holland

Stefanie Olivola

Stephanie Eleanor Henrichs Welch

Stewart Mack

Vince Fairclough